VOYAGE OF MAGIC & MALICE

Vampires of Charleston Book 3

Madalyn Rae

content warning

This book contains immortal children (vampire children), the death of a child, and several hints of child abuse. If any of these concepts trigger you, this might not be the book for you.

a witch, a vampire, and a book

WALKING DOWNTOWN IN CHARLESTON, South Carolina, is one of my favorite ways to pass the time. It amuses me to watch the humans and their response to the energy they feel from the vampire in their vicinity. Most don't notice, and the few who do aren't sure what they feel. Some take a wider berth as they near me, while others stare in confusion. Today, I don't pay much attention to them. It's not a leisure stroll. Today, we're going to the city library to recover the grimoire of my long-deceased baby brother, Aaron Abernathy.

The man who I've loved for over three hundred years and who sacrificed his humanity to be with me walks by my side. Double the vampires means double the stares and confusion. Captain Hawthorne Rex opens the door to the city library, following me inside.

The smell of old books smacks me in the face, making me smile.

Growing up in Scotland in the 1700s, my family was poor, which meant I wasn't afforded the luxury of books or even a formal education. My mother was my tutor, and although she did the best she could while also caring for my eight brothers and sisters, most of my time was spent helping my father on the farm or taking care of my younger siblings.

"I hate the smell of moldy books," Thorne says, covering his nose slightly.

"You're a heathen." I smile teasingly with my words. "Old book smell is one of my favorites. That and O negative."

We work our way to the large desk centered in the middle of the room. The elderly woman behind the counter is busy scanning a pile of books into a computer that looks nearly as old as she is. Where most humans stare at the vampires in front of them, this woman is oblivious.

I clear my throat loudly. "Excuse me."

"I'll be with you shortly," she answers, never looking away from her stack.

As she continues to work, the bundle of white hair piled on top of her head shakes with her movements. A pair of wire-rimmed glasses hangs precariously from her neck, the obvious victim of years of abuse and victimization of books slamming on top of them, and the knit cardigan she's wearing is the casualty of more than a few moth attacks.

She scans the last book before turning toward the two of us. "Well, aren't you a handsome thing?" She smiles, ignoring me and zooming in on the tall, dark-haired captain next to me.

Thorne turns on the charm, along with a thick Southern accent. "Why, thank you, ma'am. You're quite lovely yourself."

Pink covers her fair cheeks, and the smile that follows is mesmerizing. "Oh, stop it some more." She steps closer to the vampire. "What can I help you with, handsome?"

"We were hoping to gain access to the files in the basement," I answer.

The librarian turns toward me as if she's noticed my presence for the first time. Her disapproving eyes take in every detail of my face, no doubt sizing up her competition. "What's in the basement that interests you?" she directs her question toward the Southern gentleman at my side.

"I believe there is a book that was left in the care of the library by one of my ancestors," I answer, throwing the woman off her ancient game once more.

"I can't help you." She turns, heading toward another stack of books.

"Excuse me, ma'am," Thorne says. "The book was left in the library's care in hopes that an ancestor would be found. Elsbeth is that ancestor."

"Is that a hint of an accent other than Charleston I hear sneaking through?" she asks, turning her eyes back to Thorne, a smile once again covering her face.

"Yes, ma'am, it is. My family came from Scotland."

"Scotland." She closes her eyes. "I've always dreamed of visiting the UK. Scotland, Ireland, all the *lands*."

"It's beautiful country," I interrupt.

She sighs, clearly annoyed by the sound of my voice. "Who told you about the book?"

Pulling the letter sent from the law office intern, informing me about my brother's grimoire, from my pocket, I read the name aloud. "Abigail Orcutt."

Her face changes in an instant. "Abbi sent you?"

"Yes, ma'am." I copy Thorne's Southern style, hoping to gain her trust.

"What's your name, girl?"

"Elsbeth Abernathy. Aaron Abernathy was my...my ancestor."

It's clear from the look on her face that she knows exactly who and what I'm talking about. "I can't help you."

"Miss?"

"Allen," she answers. "Phyllis Allen."

"Ms. Allen, I need to get my hands on that book."

Phyllis reaches under the counter, handing me a stack of papers. "Fill these out, get them approved by the city, and then we'll talk."

"I'm afraid we don't have that much time," Thorne answers for both of us.

The older woman shrugs. "I'm sorry. My hands are tied. You know...bureaucracy."

"Phyllis?" She turns toward me. I focus on her eyes. "We need access to the basement now."

"You need access to the basement now," she repeats.

"You're going to allow us inside to retrieve the book," I continue the compulsion. Phyllis stares blankly into my eyes. "You're going to allow us inside to retrieve the book," I repeat.

"Like hell I am."

Thorne and I share a look. For the first time since becoming a vampire, my compulsion doesn't work. "Ms. Phyllis." Thorne takes over, turning on the charm. She looks into his eyes. "Maybe you misunderstood. You're going to allow us inside the basement to retrieve Elsbeth's book."

"Damn, your eyes are more convincing than hers, but again, no." She glances between us. "You vampires think you can control everyone, don't you?"

"I'm not sure what you're talking about," Thorne answers.

"Don't bullshit me, son. You're a vampire." She sniffs in my direction. "So are you." Pursing her lips, she makes a disapproving noise. "I hoped you were different. Can't say I'm not disappointed."

"What do you know about vampires?" I ask the aging librarian.

"Other than they're condescending assholes with a god complex who think they can get whatever they want by confusing a person's mind—not much." Thin arms cross in front of her chest. "Oh, they drink human blood, leaving their victims dead when they're done."

"Ms. Phyllis, I can assure you, neither of us drinks human blood." At Thorn's words, the aftertaste of goat's blood fills my palate. I'd much prefer human blood, and Ms. Phyllis is correct. Over the three hundred years I've been a vampire, I've killed countless humans for nothing more than the sustenance they provide.

"Young man, do I look that dumb?"

"No, ma'am," he answers without hesitation.

"How did it not work on you?" I ask the elderly woman.

Phyllis shrugs. "Skills." She leans in closer. "What do you want with Aaron's book?"

"Do you know what kind of book it is?"

Phyllis swipes her hand across a thick book on the desk. The cover lifts, opening to the first page. "I know quite a bit more than most would think."

"You're a witch." Thorne's words are more of a statement than a question.

"I knew you were more than just a pretty face." Phyllis turns back to me. "I'll ask again. What do you want with Aaron's book?"

"Aaron wanted me to have it. It's his grimoire," I whisper the last part of my statement.

"Why would a powerful warlock leave his grimoire to a vampire? A grimoire like Aaron's in the wrong hands could be deadly. Aaron Abernathy has been dead for over two centuries. I'm going to need more proof than your word that you are who you say you are."

I drag my only picture ID from my back pocket, setting it on the countertop. "Elsbeth Abernathy." I point to my name, typed neatly across the card.

Phyllis picks the ID up and slides the wire-rimmed glasses onto her nose. "Says here you were born in the year 2000."

"Give or take a few centuries."

She nods at the stack of papers in my hand. "Fill those out. You should hear something within six to eight weeks." The woman turns, heading back to the stack of books.

"Aaron Abernathy was my youngest brother. I was taken from the ship hired to bring us from Scotland to Charles Town, South Carolina, in 1715. I was nineteen years old. The last time I saw him, Aaron was nothing more than an infant."

Phyllis looks at me like a child at story time. "I'm listening."

"The man who took me was a pirate, but not just any pirate—a vampire pirate. He turned me into this." I take a deep breath, willing the memories of that time to stay at bay. "I am asking nicely, Ms. Phyllis, for you to please give us access to what is rightfully mine."

The librarian stares into my eyes longer than necessary. She moves slowly across the circulation desk, sliding a hidden door up and exiting in front of us. Thorne and I watch as she moves toward a solid wood wall before turning to face us. "Well...are you coming or not?"

We're behind her seconds later as she pushes an invisible space on the wall, releasing a door that sits flush. Phyllis leads us through several small rooms full of wooden filing cabinets to a spiral staircase. "Watch your step," she commands, descending the metal stairs slowly. "We've lost some good people to these stairs throughout the years."

Twenty-three steps later, we're greeted with black-and-white checkerboard tiles. Phyllis pushes an old switch on the wall, filling the room with ambient light. "This is it. The archives."

Lining the walls and every four feet inside are bookshelves covered with everything from books to boxes to papers. "This is overwhelming," I say, not realizing I spoke my words aloud.

"Yeah. That's why Abigail was here." She works her way through the room to the table in the far corner. Phyllis takes a deep breath before placing her hand on top of an antique wooden box. "By time and secret hand concealed, I call the lock to now be healed. Two hundred years, no more to bind, reveal the treasure, lost to time. Open now, by light and will, this ancient box, its secrets spill." The box opens on cue, and Phyllis reaches in, pulling out a book that's much larger than I expected.

Pushing a stack of newspapers to the side, she sets the book on the now clean table. The cloth covering the grimoire looks as if it were wrapped yesterday, not two centuries ago. "I was able to open the container, but only Aaron's intended recipient will be able to open the book. I am just the guardian. The book will know the truth of who you are."

I move toward the leather-bound relic. A large symbol covers the front, surrounded by scraps of fabric. "What does this mean?" I ask.

"It's a rune. Aaron's magic was widely based on them."

"What does it mean?"

"Love," Phyllis answers simply.

"How do I open it?"

"I don't know. Each grimoire is different, and each craft is special."

I step closer to the book, running my fingers over the imprint. The intricacy of the leatherwork is beautiful. Imagining my baby brother designing and making the cover sends chill bumps down my spine.

"Place your hand on it," Thorne says through our silent connection.

Following instructions, I place my open palm on top of the rune. Energy rushes me as the bindings wrapped around the cover release and disappear before my eyes. "Did I do that?"

"Yes, you did," Phyllis answers. "Holy shit. You are Elsbeth Abernathy, the long-lost sister of Aaron Abernathy."

"Aye," I answer, dropping the Southern charm.

"Take the book," she says. "It's rightfully yours."

Lifting the book from the ancient box, the energy that's inside fills me with a feeling that matches the rune on the front—love. Tears fill my eyes as emotions overwhelm me. "Thank you, Ms. Phyllis." I fight to keep my emotions at bay.

"Of course. I hope you'll forgive me for my skepticism. It's been my job to protect the grimoire for fifty years, as it was for the women who came before me."

"Thank you."

Phyllis moves to the bottom of the stairs. "I believe you'll find something meant for you inside. I'll leave you to it."

Her heels click on the metal stairs as she works her way back to the main floor of the library, leaving Thorne and me alone with my baby brother's grimoire.

"This is it. Aaron's grimoire," I speak the words out loud. Thorne lays a protective hand on my shoulder. "It's the only physical tie I have to any of them."

"Aye," he answers. "I'm going to give you some privacy." He places a warm kiss on my head before moving in the same direction Phyllis did moments earlier.

I take a deep breath before pulling the heavy cover open. Inside is a folded piece of parchment, sealed with a red stamp and my name written in perfect script. Breaking the seal, I open the letter.

To My Lost Sister,

In death, there is clarity. The years that once stood between us, veiled in shadow and silence, have unfolded before me. I see now what I could not have known in life—the fate you endured, the curse placed upon our family, and the unspeakable horrors you faced on that wretched ship.

You were taken when I was just an infant, snatched from our family by a monster that walked under the guise of a man—a pirate with fangs and a hunger for blood. I never had the chance to know you, yet I have spent my entire life chasing the memory of a sister I was too young to remember. Even now, from the land of the dead, I feel the echo of our shared bloodline vibrating across the centuries.

They told me stories of you, whispers in the night when they thought I couldn't hear.

Stories of your beauty, your laughter, and the promise of a life you might have led. But your fate was stolen from you, ripped away by the very creature who took you from us. I cannot imagine the torment you endured or the years spent as a slave to darkness.

Though my body has long since turned to dust, I have left behind more than just memories. In the grimoire of our ancestors, I carved a spell, a tether, so that my words may reach you, even from death. It is not too late, Elsbeth. We are bound by blood and to the power we carry. The vampire may have claimed your body, but he does not own your soul.

I am with you, always. Find me in the wind, in the flame, in the whispers of the moon. You are not lost. You were never lost to me.

In the shadows,
Aaron Abernathy

An undeniable hunger fills my body. Not a hunger for food, but for the love that was denied. A hunger for the family I never grew old with. Kragen is dead, but he took much more than my humanity while he walked the earth.

I spend more time than necessary running my fingers over the intricate design on the cover. "Thank you, Aaron. I regret I never had the chance to know you."

Energy flows through me as I slowly ascend the stairs, hugging the grimoire to my chest. I can't hide my smirk at seeing the look on Thorne's face. Phyllis has him cornered and is telling him a story from her youth. On the outside, he looks interested. On the inside, he's miserable.

"There she is," Phyllis says, greeting me with a nod. "I hope you found what you were looking for."

"I did. Thank you."

Thorne takes my hand into his, and we turn toward the exit. "Elsbeth?" the librarian calls. "There's a reason that grimoire has been protected for two hundred years, and it has nothing to do with you. There are *people* more powerful than either of us who would love to lay claim to the grimoire of Aaron Abernathy. Guard it with your life."

......

Thorne reads through Aaron's letter for the second time while I continue admiring the artistry on the cover. "This is a beautiful letter, acushla."

"Aye. I wish I could've known him." Thorne wipes a stray tear from my cheek. "I don't know what to do with these spells." I pull the grimoire to my chest, hugging it tightly. "I'm not a witch. I'm just a vampire with a bad attitude."

"I think we all have a little magic in us." Thorne folds Aaron's letter, placing it gently inside the envelope. "Maybe some know how to access it better than others."

My phone buzzes, drawing my attention away from the grimoire and to the text sent from Celeste.

Brayden woke up.

Sliding my phone back into my pocket, I don't bother responding. The immortal children Eudora captured have been all I've thought about for the past month. Worrying about Alex, Autumn, and Everly, and what the Goddess of the Sea wants with them, has been my priority since returning to Charleston. As a human, Brayden exhibited more power than any of the *special* immortal children. Now, as a vampire, there's no limit to his abilities. Anger fills me, thinking about the boy not having a choice in his future. He can't be older than seven or eight, and now he's a vampire. His life was stolen from him, the same as mine.

"Brayden's awake," I relay the text to Thorne.

"What's next?" he asks.

"For him or everyone else?" Anger fills my words.

Thorne sits next to me on the overstuffed couch. "There wasn't a choice, acushla."

"There's always a choice, Thorne. His life was stolen from him."

"His life was over with his parents' accident. He would've died."

"But it would've been his choice." My words are dumb. Brayden never had a choice. "What's he going to do? Turn into a vampire that may or may not kill everyone he comes in contact with and magically help find Alex and the girls?"

"Yes." Thorne's words are straightforward.

"They may not even be alive."

"Even if they're not alive, Eudora and Marnie are. That's something that needs to end. Even with our added abilities, we're not strong enough to defeat a goddess and a demigod. Luna's death is proof of that." His words hit hard as the image of Luna flashes to mind.

"What are you suggesting?"

"I'm suggesting we put an end to this once and for all."

"How?" I wipe a stray tear.

"Brayden's awake. Let's go see if he's eating everyone or in control." Thorne's words mean going back to New Orleans.

"Okay."

seriously?

THORNE PULLS the rental car to a stop in front of the three-story home in the Garden District of New Orleans. The last time we were here, the windows were blown out, and most of the yard was destroyed. Sitting in front of the home now, there's no evidence of the demigod Marnie's path of destruction. In fact, the house looks better than I remember.

"I feel him," I whisper.

"Aye, me, too. His energy feels different than before. Why isn't he shielding it?"

I take a deep breath. "This is going to be a shit show." My mind flashes back to Brayden, the human, and the *special* abilities he had even then. Without any effort, he was able to shield energy, meaning he could make anyone invisible—even the strongest of vampires. Along with being a human shield, he was able to strengthen other *special* vampires' powers—special vampires like Alex and the girls. Those are just the two that we know about. Now that he's a vampire, I have a feeling his power will be limitless.

The door opens before Thorne has the chance to knock. Standing in the doorframe is a boy who was human the last time I saw him. His skin is flawless, and his soft blonde hair is perfectly combed. "Hello, Captain Thorne." He holds his hand toward Thorne, who shakes it, not sure what else to do. Brayden turns to me. "Hello, Elsbeth."

"Hi, Brayden. How are you?"

"I'm well, thank you. Did you know I'm a vampire now?"

"We...we did." I look past him, hoping to spot Fran, Celeste, or Amelia...someone—anyone.

"Amelia and Celeste went home. Fran is upstairs."

"Did you read my mind, Brayden?"

He wrinkles his forehead. "I don't think so. You thought it at me, and I heard it."

"Elsie, Thorne!" Fran rushes down the stairs toward us. "Come in, please."

Thorne follows me inside the flawlessly decorated home. My eyes find the spot where my friend took her last breath, where Luna sacrificed her life to save the immortal children. There are no remnants of her. Nothing to mark the spot where she died. It's as if she never existed. Fran follows my line of sight. "I'm sorry, Elsie."

"How is he?" I ask, pushing the thoughts of her death from my mind.

"I'm perfect, aren't I, Fran?" Brayden answers the question for the older vampire.

"Yes, you are, dear," she agrees, wrapping an arm around his shoulders.

"How are you in control so quickly?" I ask whoever answers first.

Brayden shrugs. "It was easy."

I share a look with Thorne. I'm not sure I'm buying his performance, but he seems more in control than I expected. "What are you eating, Brayden?"

"Goat's blood," he answers. "It's not great, but it works."

I laugh. "That, we can agree on."

"I'm not complaining that you're here, but to what do we owe the pleasure of your visit? Do you have any news of the children?" Fran asks, keeping her arm protectively around Brayden.

"They're here because of me," the boy answers. "They wanted to see if I was in control."

"Are you?" Thorne asks.

"What do you think, Captain?"

"I think you seem in control, but the history of what you are says you're not."

Brayden crosses his arms in defiance. "I can assure you I am perfectly in control. I'm me but better."

"I can see that," Thorne answers, trying to keep the peace.

"Where are Amelia and Celeste?" I try changing the subject.

"Amelia has her own life to live. She and Topher are busy with pack affairs, and Celeste went back to Mississippi."

"They felt safe leaving Brayden alone with you?"

"Why shouldn't they?" the boy answers once again. His arrogance is off-putting. He is highly talented, but his body language and attitude are digging deep into my skin. Human Brayden was much easier to empathize with. Vampire Brayden is a little asshole.

"Brayden, would you excuse us for a minute?" Fran hugs his shoulders tightly, dismissing him to his room.

He glares at me, clearly reading my thoughts before sighing loudly and moving up the stairs, stopping where Luna took her last breath. For a brief moment, I swear he smirks at the memory of her death.

I stare at the blonde-haired immortal child until he makes his way completely up the stairs. Fran silently moves through the pocket door that leads to her office, returning seconds later carrying an electronic device that reminds me of a remote control. Placing it on the landing of the stairs, she pushes a button and moves in front of us.

"You can speak and think freely, now."

Thorne shares the same look as I feel. "What are you talking about, Fran?"

"That device produces a shield. It scrambles brainwave frequencies, making it impossible to *hear* our conversations."

"How is that possible?" Thorne asks.

"I started building it while Brayden was still in the hospital. It's a simple device, really. It..."

"Fran," I interrupt. "Why do you need to block him from hearing us? What aren't you telling us?"

"He's doing great, but he's not ready to know everything."

"The whole damn reason Celeste *altered* him was for him to help find the others. If you're going to protect him, he might as well have died with his parents." My words are cruel, and I immediately feel guilty.

Fran glances at the staircase, doubting her ingenuity. "We have bigger fish to fry than Brayden or the children at the moment."

"What could be bigger than saving Alex and the girls?" Thorne asks the question of the day.

"I was contacted by the local coven."

I feel my forehead wrinkle. "Coven? As in a witches' coven?"

"Yes. They had some concerns and contacted me."

"Okay." As far as I know, there are only two people who know I have Aaron's grimoire—Thorne and Phyllis. Fran has no idea my youngest brother was a warlock, but I've learned over the years that there are no coincidences.

"What were their concerns?" Thorne asks, sensing my turmoil.

"Brayden," she answers. "They want him under protection."

"Why would a coven of witches want an immortal vampire child under protection?" I ask.

"Because the power he holds can only have come from one place. His bloodline."

"They think he's a witch?" Thorne asks.

"That's exactly what they think."

"He's a vampire, living with a vampire nanny. How much more protection does he need?" I don't know why I'm annoyed.

"For now, that's fine. However, in the future, there could be more needed."

Thorne crosses his arms at his chest. "Nothing personal, Fran. But what the witches want or need isn't our concern."

"We came to check on Brayden, not to be involved in anything other than that." My voice sounds tired, even for a vampire. My phone buzzes, drawing my attention.

> Brayden's still unconscious. I'll let you know when he wakes.

I stare at my phone, confused by Celeste's message. *"What does this mean?"* I flash the message at Thorne, who looks equally confused.

"I'm pleased to hear you're not interested in being involved elsewhere." Fran's voice changes timbre as she stands a little taller.

"What are you talking about, Fran?" I stare at the elderly vampire. Her normally white hair begins to change hues, turning darker before my eyes.

"Fran?" Thorne asks, moving closer to my side. "What's going on?"

Where Fran stood moments earlier, a much younger woman stands. Her hair is long and dark, and her copper eyes sparkle with mischief. *"What the hell?"* Thorne asks through my mind.

The woman turns toward Thorne. "Not hell, Mr. Rex—New Orleans." The smile that covers her face reminds me of the Cat Alice met in Wonderland.

The house surrounding us begins to transform from the familiarity of Fran's warm abode to a building resembling a warehouse. Warm colors and comfortable furniture are replaced with the cold steel of a metal building.

"What is this?" I ask the woman in front of me. "An illusion?"

"You could call it that. We prefer to use the term 'veil of shadows.'"

"Whatever the hell you call it, what did you do to Fran and Brayden?" Anger fills my words.

"I can assure you, neither was harmed. We did nothing to them."

"You know what we are. You know what we can do. You're either dumb or want to die." Energy forms in my core with my words.

"Elsbeth Abernathy, I am well aware of your abilities." She glances at Thorne. "However, you hold no power here. You cannot harm me."

I accept her invitation and stare at the woman in front of me. In an instant, I'm inches from her face, wearing the face of a monster. "We're leaving."

"You are free to leave anytime you choose." The smug smile on her face makes me want to drain her blood. A desire I've kept at bay for months.

I turn, passing Thorne as the two of us move toward the exit. "Oh, one more thing." We turn back, staring at the petite woman from across the warehouse. "If you want to see the boy or the old lady again, give me the grimoire."

Hairs on the back of my neck stand at attention. Shit. I work to keep my face neutral. "I don't know what you're talking about."

"Don't insult my intelligence, vampire. I know who you are. I know who your brother was, and I know what is now in your possession."

"Then you should also know that I hold his power inside of me," I lie.

The cackle from the witch reminds me of cartoons I've watched featuring the personification of a witch. "You don't have the power to contain the grimoire. Whatever delusion led you to that belief is wrong."

"We're done here." Thorne kicks the barred door, knocking it off its hinges and opening the door to the outside. Both of us stop in our tracks at the view on the other side.

"What is this?" Thorne asks out loud. "Are we in Charleston?"

"Aye," I answer in confusion. The cityscape in front of us is full of steeples and the familiar landscape of our home.

"How is this possible?"

"Maybe you didn't understand the first time. I'll give you the benefit of the doubt and simplify it slightly." The witch is in front of us from seemingly nowhere. "Veil of shadows," she uses a darker woo-woo voice, wiggling her hands to the sides. "Does that help?"

"No," I answer truthfully. "We flew on an airplane to New Orleans. How did you do this?"

"You never went anywhere," she answers simply. "It was nothing more than…"

"A veil of shadows." Thorne fills in the blanks.

"See, he gets it."

"Who are you?" I ask for the first time.

"Who I am is of no concern. However, I'm feeling generous. You may call me Sable."

"Like the color?" My smart mouth shows itself again.

"More like the animal." She holds her hands in front of her body. "This is your last chance. The boy and the old woman will die. Give me the grimoire."

"Do you think I have it in my pocket? I left it in the car," I lie again. "Oops, that means it's in New Orleans. Or maybe not, since we're not in New Orleans. Shouldn't you know the answer to that?"

My words anger Sable. She steps closer, holding her hands to the side. "If I snap my fingers, they will die."

"Okay, Thanos," I retort. "He's a vampire and being protected by a vampire."

She transforms into the image of Fran. "This is the woman protecting him? Were you curious how I was able to imitate her so easily?"

"Where is she?"

Sable sighs, clearly annoyed with my ignorance. Thorne takes advantage of her distraction, rushing toward her like a linebacker. He's moving faster than human eyes can track, yet the witch moves at just the right time, stepping out of his way.

"I snap, and they're dead," Sable repeats.

A loud metal sound explodes through the Charleston cityscape. "Stop!" a deep voice echoes through the room. "Don't listen to her. Fran and the child are safe."

I turn, finding the source of the voice. A man stands not far behind Thorne and me. He's at least a head taller than me, and lycanthrope energy pours from him.

"What are you doing here, wolf?" Sable asks.

"Leave before I make you leave, witch."

A wicked grin covers her face. "You're alone and naïve. What can a wolf and two vamps do to me?"

"You're about to find out," he warns.

Sable smiles and disappears before my eyes, leaving the three of us staring at each other in confusion. "What was that?"

"That was Sable Arden, the leader of a rogue group of witches from New Orleans. They've been trying to gain power through the use of dark magic."

"How are you involved?" Thorne asks.

"It's my job. Some lycan get to be the alpha, some get to be the brains behind the alpha. I'll let you figure out which I am." He smiles, stepping closer and offering his hand to Thorne. "It's a pleasure to meet you both. I've heard so much about you. I feel like I already know you. I'm Cameron St. James. I believe you know my brother, Christopher, and his wife, Amelia."

power from beyond

I STARE at the giant lycanthrope, seeing the resemblance between him and Topher. They share the same dark hair and the same bright green eyes. Where Topher has a more rigid jawline and scruffy beard, Cameron's jawline is softer and home to neatly trimmed facial hair.

"Explain this," Thorne says. "How the hell did she make us think we flew to New Orleans?"

"It's what they do," Cameron answers. "Spells are amazing things. Especially spells from powerful casters like Sable."

"To be clear, we're still in Charleston?" I'm still not sure I know what to believe.

"You are."

"If you're Topher's brother, why are you here, in Charleston?" Thorne asks.

"It's my job," he repeats. "I'm guessing you figured

out I'm the brains behind the alpha?" He smiles warmly, easing the tension. "Topher sent me to help the Charleston pack. The future Alpha has stepped away from his duties for a while, and the Alpha requested help from the New Orleans pack."

"Micah stepped away?" My heart sinks, thinking about Luna and the connection they formed before her death.

"He did. Connor needed someone to step into his position for a few weeks. That person is me."

"How do you know Sable?"

Dark eyebrows raise. "Part of my position with the pack is dealing with the local covens. Most work well with the paranormal community. Occasionally, we run across a group that doesn't."

"I'm guessing Sable's in one of the groups that doesn't work well," Thorne says.

"You'd be guessing correctly." Cameron's energy is light and easy. "Sable's group seeks power through darkness. She's powerful, ruthless, and will stop at nothing to get what they want."

Thorne and I share a look. "She's after my brother's grimoire."

Cam raises his eyebrows. "Your brother was a witch?"

"He was a warlock. To be honest, I don't know if they're the same thing or not." I sigh, feeling very uneducated. "My brother was Aaron Abernathy." The lycanthrope lifts one side of his mouth higher than the other.

A move I've witnessed Topher perform a few times. "Have you heard of him?"

"Legends of Aaron Abernathy have passed through the paranormal community for centuries. He was one of the most powerful practitioners to live in Charleston and New Orleans. Hell, to live in America." Tears fill my eyes with Cameron's words. "He never had children of his own, which is how grimoire magic is usually passed down. Through research on Aaron and the coven, I determined the reality of his grimoire, but was never able to locate it." He pauses, crossing his arms in front of his chest.

"Why are lycan interested in witch business?" Thorne asks.

"Interested isn't exactly the word. My job is more of a liaison between the worlds. My job is to assess a situation and advise as needed." Cam's muscles move slightly as he stares at the two of us. "Can I ask where you found it?"

"It was being guarded by an older witch." I'm not willing to give every detail to a man I just met. Topher's brother or not, I don't know him well enough to divulge information about Ms. Phyllis.

"It was Phyllis, wasn't it?" he asks, surprising me. "I knew that old bat had it the whole time." He runs a hand through his hair. "Damn, she was sneaky. Where is it now?" He looks around.

Alarms ring through my mind. "It's safe," Thorne answers. *"Call Topher, now."*

Thorne shares the same concern. Pulling my phone from my pocket, I pretend to have a call. "If you'll excuse me. I need to answer this." Stepping out of the warehouse, I move away from the building at vampire speed.

"I'll keep him busy."

Pulling up my contact list, I search for Topher's number. I finally find it listed under *Alpha T*, and my thoughts immediately turn to Luna, who added his information to my phone. I push the sadness away and call the number listed. He answers on the first ring.

"Elsie?"

"Yeah, it's me."

Topher laughs deeply. *"I wasn't sure who this was. Your name is listed as 'Bitchy Vampire' in my contacts."*

I laugh with him. *"Luna must've added our numbers to each other's phones. I'll admit, she wasn't wrong with the bitchy part."*

"How can I help you, Elsie?"

"Cameron?"

He pauses. *"Cameron? I'm not sure what you're asking."*

"Your brother, Cameron. Is he in Charleston?"

"Yeah. I sent him a few days ago. Is everything okay?"

I sigh, not sure how to answer. *"Can you find where he is right now?"*

"Sure. Let me hang up, and I'll call him."

"Perfect. Thank you." I hang up the phone, not sure

what to think about everything. Several minutes pass before he texts back.

> He's at a lycan bar on Broad Street. I just spoke to him.

Shit! The sound of crashing metal echoes off the buildings behind me as I slide my phone back into my jeans. I don't bother responding to Topher before returning to the warehouse. The door is standing open, and the room is silent. *"Thorne!"* I call through our connection.

"Outside," he answers. I run through the warehouse, exiting the other side into a group of overgrown trees.

"Where?" The sound of limbs breaking draws my attention and sends me moving toward what I imagine is a fight between Thorne and the veil of shadows.

I arrive just as Thorne is thrown into the air, slamming against the thick trunk of an ancient tree. In front of me stands Sable, the woman from before. She's all of five feet tall and looks more like a soccer mom than someone capable of throwing a three-hundred-year-old vampire anywhere.

"Hey!" I yell, drawing her attention to me.

"Where's the grimoire, Elsie?" she asks, stalking closer.

"It's safe." My words are a lie. It's sitting on a bed at our temporary house in Charleston. Phyllis warned me there were powerful people after it. I had no idea she meant this.

"I will not hesitate to kill him."

"That was a lucky blow," Thorne says, back at my side. "I can assure you, it won't happen again."

A deep growl echoes off the trees. Without turning, I know the real Cameron St. James is the source. The energy I associate with Topher rushes me. How could I have been stupid enough to believe the facade she cast? Beside me, a dark brown wolf stands tall. The arch of his back is level with my shoulders, and angry energy rolls from him. The three of us stare down the tiny woman while energy forms in my core, begging to be released.

"You will die," Thorne warns. Cameron growls in agreement.

"Burn," I say the word aloud that killed my maker, Kragen, not long ago. On demand, lightning strikes the tree behind Sable, igniting it instantly. "You're next," I warn. The tiny woman smirks and disappears, leaving no trace of her ever being there.

"Is she gone for real this time?" I ask the men on either side of me.

"Aye. I think so." Thorne turns to our lycanthrope guest. "Cameron St. James?" The wolf howls in response before running into the woods.

"What the hell is going on?" I ask Thorne. "I don't know who or what to believe at this point."

"Aye, me either."

Seconds later, the man we thought we met earlier walks out of the woods completely naked. "Hi." He waves. "I'm Cam. Topher told me you might need help."

"How'd you find us?" I ask, trying to detour my eyes from the obvious. "When I spoke to Topher, he said you were on Broad Street."

"I smelled you," he answers simply, pointing toward town. "Besides, Broad Street is just over there." I glance in the direction he's pointing. He's right. It wouldn't take a human long to get here, let alone a lycanthrope.

"Thank you."

"I didn't do anything." He looks between the two of us. "Which one of you did the tree thing?"

"That was me," I answer truthfully.

Cam laughs. "That was awesome! I've never seen a vampire do that before."

"That's probably a good thing," Thorne answers for me.

"What did she want?"

"A very important book," I answer, not willing to share more information. That lesson was learned quickly.

"She seemed...determined."

"Yeah," Thorne agrees. He moves toward the lycanthrope. "Thank you, Cameron, for your help."

"Please, call me Cam. My mom called me Cameron when I was in trouble." He chuckles with his answer.

"Thank you, Cam."

"Anytime." He turns, leaving the two of us in the

woods. His bare ass shines as he walks away, clearly not giving a shit. His carefree attitude makes me laugh.

"Why do I feel like that's on purpose?" Thorne asks, laughing with me.

"Because you're right." Turning toward the man I love, I say, "I want to go to the library."

"Aye, that's exactly what I was thinking. Ms. Phyllis is the only person we can trust right now. At least, I think we can trust her." We move vampire speed through the woods and into downtown Charleston. We're standing in front of the double doors of the brick library within minutes.

A blast of cool air hits me in the face as we enter the quiet building. Ms. Phyllis turns from her stack of books as soon as we enter, no doubt sensing our energy. "The library's closed," she announces loudly while making eye contact with me. Her voice echoes through the crowded room. "Leave your books where they are and get out now. There's a gas leak."

Following her orders, patrons drop their books, heading toward the doors immediately. Phyllis moves from her perch at the circulation desk and in front of us. The last human exits, and she locks the door behind him. "What's happened?" she asks, looking us up and down. "Did you lose the grimoire?"

"No," I answer truthfully.

"Then why are you here?"

"Sable Arden."

Phyllis sighs deeply. "Shit. How did that bitch find you?"

"We don't know, but she did," Thorne answers.

"She knew things she shouldn't know. Vampire things," I add.

"Like what?" Phyllis moves toward an empty table, pulling a chair out to sit.

Thorne and I share a look. "She cast some sort of spell to make us think we flew to New Orleans to visit a friend of ours. She called it the..."

"The veil of shadows," Phyllis interrupts.

"Yeah."

"How did you uncover the veil?"

"What do you mean?" Thorne asks.

"What made you realize it wasn't real?"

"She dropped her disguise, well, one of them. It's a long story." I rub my temples, not sure how to explain what happened. "What didn't you tell me?"

"I warned you there were people more powerful than you who would love to have his grimoire."

"You did, but I thought you meant metaphorically."

Phyllis laughs at my words. "I may be a librarian, but my words are not flowery." She stands, propping her hands on her hips and walking around in a small circle. "How the hell did Sable find you so quickly?"

"Who else knows I have it?"

"No one."

I stalk closer to the witch. "That's not the truth, is it?"

Phyllis stops walking, looking me in the eyes. "Young lady. If you think for one minute that I had anything to do with the knowledge of you or that book getting to Sable, you couldn't be more wrong. I've dedicated my life to the protection of it and kept it hidden for nearly as long."

I sigh. "What are we up against?"

"Sable is powerful and crazy, which, in my book, is a lethal combination."

"What does she want with the grimoire?" Thorne asks.

"Aaron Abernathy was a powerful warlock. She wants what others have wanted before—his power."

Remembering what Cameron or Sable, or hell—I don't know— said, I ask the question that's been on my mind ever since. "Was Aaron into dark magic?"

Phyllis sighs while straightening the few buttons on her dress. "There is no such thing as dark magic. Most people get that wrong. Dark and light magic aren't opposites. They're simply two sides of the same coin. The magic itself doesn't change, only the intent behind it. Both can heal, protect, or destroy, depending on how they're wielded. 'Dark magic' is feared because it's often used for personal gain or control, but so is 'light magic' when someone casts a love spell or bends fate to their will. What truly matters is the heart of the witch casting the spell. Magic is neutral—just energy waiting to be shaped. Whether it's called light or dark, it's all the same force flowing through us. It's our choices and our desires that give it meaning. So, to answer your question, Aaron was not into dark or light magic. He was simply into magic."

"She's not going to stop, is she?" I ask.

"No, she won't. Not until she has the grimoire or dies trying."

"How can we stop her?" Thorne asks.

"Use what's inside of you," Phyllis answers. "Both of you. There's magical power inside you. I felt it the moment you entered the library."

Thorne and I share a look. "What do you mean?" he asks.

"I mean, both of you hold magic in your blood." Phyllis turns toward me. "Hell, Aaron Abernathy was your brother, for goddess's sake. It wouldn't make sense that he would be the only one with power. Harness the power, use it, and take what is rightfully yours."

"How?" I ask. My words are no louder than a whisper.

"That's what you've got to figure out."

"Can you help us?" Thorne asks for the two of us.

Phyllis laughs. "Child, I'm old. I'll do my best, but I'm not promising anything."

"That's all we can ask for," he answers.

"Tell her," I urge through our connection.

"Elsie and I are what others call *special,*" he admits to the witch.

"Special, how?"

"We can communicate with each other telepathically," I admit.

"I don't know much about vampires, but is that not normal?"

"No, ma'am," Thorne answers.

"Is that all?" Phyllis asks.

"I burned my maker by telling him to burn."

"Explain." The librarian wrinkles her nose.

I shrug. "I don't know how I did it or what caused it. I told him to burn, and he did."

Phyllis crosses her arms across her chest. "No doubt, turning into a vampire enhanced your abilities." She turns toward Thorne. "There's no denying Elsie's talented. I can feel the power flowing from her. But you, Thorne, are the powerful one. Magic runs through you —ancient magic."

"Me?"

"Yes, you. The power that runs through your blood is old, wise, and dangerous."

Thorne shifts awkwardly from foot to foot. "Can we start now?" I ask, taking the attention off him.

She holds her empty wrist up dramatically, staring at an invisible watch. "Well, shit. I'll have to cancel my date." She winks with her words.

the spell of all spells

BEFORE LEAVING THE LIBRARY, I program the address of the home where we're staying into Ms. Phyllis's phone. A few minutes after we arrive, an oversized SUV slows down, stopping in front of the house. The small woman slides out of the driver's seat, making me laugh. Her size in comparison to her mode of transportation is comedic.

"What do you think?" I ask the stoic vampire next to me.

"About what?"

"Seriously?" I scoff. "What Phyllis said about the power in your blood?"

He shrugs. "I don't know if I believe it."

"I do," I answer as Phyllis makes her way into the small yard.

Thorne doesn't respond. Instead, he offers his arm

to the elderly witch. I follow the two of them into the house, not sure why his energy has changed.

"This is beautiful," Phyllis says, running a hand over the intricately carved woodwork in the entry. "I've always loved these old colonial homes down here. The history they hold." She sucks in a deep breath. "Can you imagine what these walls would say if they could talk?"

"I'm sure they'd have a lot to say," Thorne agrees.

"Can I get you something to drink, Ms. Phyllis?" I ask.

"I'd love a water." The look on her face changes quickly. "You do have water, don't you?"

"Of course." I return a few minutes later with a glass of clear liquid. Thorne is standing in the middle of the living area with Phyllis behind him. "Close your eyes and feel within," she instructs him.

Setting her drink on a nearby table, I move to the back of the room, unsure if I should watch or join.

"Come, Elsbeth," Phyllis answers my unasked question. Following instructions, I move closer to the duo. "Close your eyes," she instructs me. "Feel the energy of the room."

I do as she suggests, letting the energy from everything surrounding us vibrate through my body. Feeling energy is something I've been able to do since before becoming a vampire. I remember several times while growing up that I was able to feel the energy from our farmland. My father sometimes would ask what the land felt like before each planting season.

Through the past few weeks, I've found it easier to draw on that ability and feel the energy surrounding me.

The power slowly forms in the pit of my stomach and works its way through my body. "That's it," Phyllis whispers. "Now let it go." I open my eyes, releasing the power into the open fireplace, setting the gas logs aflame.

"Impressive." The witch nods. "What else can you do?"

"Nothing more than communicating with Thorne telepathically."

Phyllis turns toward the captain. "What about you?"

"Compared to Elsie, nothing. I can't light anything on fire. I can't fly." He shrugs. "I'm just me."

"May I?" Phyllis asks, stepping in front of Thorne and holding her hands toward him.

"Aye." He looks confused as she places the palms of her hands on his shoulders. "Communicate with each other."

Thorne laughs through my mind. *"This seems weird."*

"Aye, it is. But I trust her."

Phyllis sucks in a deep breath. "Where is your family from?"

"Scotland," he answers, repeating the same response as the first time we met the older witch.

"All of them?" She continues.

"Aye. As far as I know. It wasn't possible to trace

your ancestry in the 18th century. What I knew was from word of mouth."

Phyllis steps away. "May I perform a spell?"

Thorne looks at me before answering. "Aye." His voice is soft.

"Elsbeth, do you have a candle?"

"I think so." Rummaging through the kitchen, I find a soft pink tapered candle. "Will this work?" I show her my discovery.

"It'll do. It's not the color but the intention." Phyllis takes the candle, lights the wick, and lets a bit of the wax drop onto a small plate before placing the base in the wax. "I need you to relax. I've never tried something like this on a vampire." She laughs at her words. "That sounded crazy to say out loud." Phyllis clears her throat. "Here we go." She takes a deep breath. "By blood and night, I call on your power, awaken the magic in this hour. From heart of dark, let it rise, witch's strength, now realize. Vampire's gift, added to flame, magic flows, speak your name."

I stare at Thorne, half expecting him to float or glow or—something. He opens his eyes, looking around the room. "Did it work?" he asks.

"We won't know," the witch answers.

"Ms. Phyllis? What's the point in that spell if we can't tell if it works?" I cross my arms across my chest, trying not to show my annoyance through body language. With my words, the candle explodes into flames, burning to the plate instantly.

"There's your answer."

"I don't feel anything," Thorne admits.

With his words, the energy in the house changes. What felt comfortable moments earlier now feels heavy, almost overwhelming. "What's happening?" I ask anyone.

A loud knock on the door makes me jump. I laugh at the irony of a vampire jumping at the sound. "There's a wolf here," Phyllis answers.

Thorne opens the door to find Cameron St. James on the other side. "I hope you don't mind. Topher told me where to find you." Unlike the last time we saw him, he's dressed and wearing a pair of skintight jeans and a rock band T-shirt that shows every ridge, muscle, and bulge.

"Hellooo," Phyllis says, moving behind Thorne. "I've always been partial to wolves."

Cam's cheeks turn a soft shade of pink as he stares at the older woman. "Thank you?"

"Are you Cam?" I ask the tall man at our door.

"Yeah," he answers.

"Don't take this the wrong way, but how can we trust that?"

Phyllis answers for the lycanthrope. "What do you feel, Thorne?"

"What do you mean?"

"I mean, what do you feel? Let his energy wash over you. Does he feel like a wolf or me?"

Thorne stands in silence, staring at the young wolf. "He feels like a lycanthrope. He feels like Topher."

"That's because I am a lycanthrope. Can I come in? I have some news about..." He cuts his words short, looking at Phyllis.

"She knows," I fill in the blanks.

"Oh!" His eyes open wide as he enters the house. "I did some digging after our meeting earlier. It seems that Sable's been in town for several days."

"Honey, she's been in and out of town for years. She's determined to get her hands on that grimoire."

"Are you after the grimoire, too?" Cam asks.

Phyllis's warm laugh fills the room. "No, dear. I'm here merely as a guide."

"Okay. That answers a ton of questions." Cam's sarcasm makes me smile.

"Don't worry. We're confused, too." I turn to Phyllis. "What do you know about Sable?"

"You might want to sit down." Thorne sits on the edge of the couch with me at his side. Cam chooses a footstool on the other side of the room while Phyllis stands in the middle of the room, reminding me of a teacher about to give a lecture. She takes a drink of water before speaking.

"Sable Arden is one of the most powerful witches alive today. She started just as everyone does, learning magic from her ancestors. Witchcraft can skip generations or be more powerful in one generation than others. With Sable, it seemed like the goddess shone on her. From early childhood, she had more power than anyone her age. As she grew, so did her powers along with a thirst for control."

"If Sable's so strong, why does she want Aaron's grimoire?" I ask.

Cam raises his hand. "I can answer that."

"Go ahead, hot stuff." Phyllis's flirting lightens the conversation.

"I don't know how much you know about Aaron Abernathy other than he was a powerful warlock," he continues.

"He was an infant the last time I saw him," I admit. "Phyllis would know more about his magic than me."

Phyllis laughs. "My job was to protect the grimoire, not to read it."

I stare at the witch. "You spent your life guarding the grimoire, but never used what was in it?"

"No, dear. If you remember, the grimoire was set so that only Aaron's sister, meaning you, could open it. Even if I'd wanted to read his grimoire, I wouldn't have been able to get inside. His magic was and is protected."

"How did you become its guardian?" Thorne asks the question of the day.

"Aaron was the founder of my coven. Since his death, my ancestors have been tasked with caring for and protecting the grimoire. It's an honor and privilege that I was happy to uphold." Phyllis takes a deep breath. "Sable's family belonged to his coven as well."

"Did she know the grimoire was under your care?" Cam asks, sliding forward in his seat.

"No one knows who the keepers are. Several have sought to find out through the years, but none have tried to take it—until now."

"Why now? Why is she trying to get her hands on his grimoire?" Thorne asks.

"Because her great-great-grandmother, Serafina, was powerful, just as Sable is. Serafina sought Aaron's power for years, challenging for leadership of the coven many times. Because of that, she, along with her future descendants, was cast out."

"Challenged him for leadership? This sounds more like a lycan story than a witch tale." Cam stands, crossing his arms across his chest.

"Agreed," Phyllis answers. "Serafina arrived from Scotland a few years after Aaron. She was a teenager when she arrived, and the two of them grew into their power together. Some say they were lovers."

"Lovers?" I repeat. The thought of my infant brother with a lover feels icky.

"As they grew, so did her selfishness and greed. She fought for control over the coven, stating she was the stronger of the two."

"That led to her banishment." Cam fills in the blank.

"That and the spell," the witch answers.

"Go on," I urge.

"Serafina created a spell that would bind and

compel supernatural creatures." Phyllis pauses, letting the information sink in.

"Paranormal creatures? You mean people like us?" Thorne asks.

"Among others. The spell even gave her dominion over other witches."

"What would be the purpose?" Cam asks, stepping closer to Phyllis.

The older witch laughs. "Imagine what kind of an army she could amass by commanding those who normally resist being bound. Serafina sought control over everyone and everything. Control like that would allow her to conquer or destroy *anyone* who stood in her way."

"Holy shit," I whisper. "Where is the spell now?"

"I'll give you three guesses, and the first two don't count."

I stand, heading straight for the table where I carelessly laid the grimoire when we left for what we thought was New Orleans. I take a deep breath, seeing the book in the same spot and position as earlier. Hugging it to my body, I carry it back into the living area. Phyllis smiles, seeing the book held tightly in my arms.

"By using his own spell, Aaron stole Serafina's binding spell and placed it inside the grimoire," Phyllis continues.

Opening the cover, I flip through the pages of perfect penmanship. "Some of these pages are blank."

"Oh, they're not blank, dear," the witch answers. "The spells are hidden. They will show themselves when needed." She makes the statement as if I should already know how the witch world works.

"Sable wants Serafina's spell," Cam says.

"Yes," Phyllis agrees. "She seeks to control all of us."

"We can't allow that to happen." Thorne stands, leaving me alone on the couch.

"I have no intention of letting that happen." I move to his side, still gripping the grimoire.

Phyllis huffs a laugh. "It's going to take more than the three of you to defeat her. She's not going to stop until she gets the spell or she's dead."

"No offense, Phyllis. You're one person, and you kept the grimoire safe for years." My words come out harsher than intended.

"Dear child, if you think I did that alone, you are mistaken. I had the power of my ancestors with me. Each spell was built on top of earlier spells, strengthening them and helping to keep the grimoire hidden. The moment the grimoire left my care, those spells were gone, and Sable was able to pinpoint the location of the book."

"Dammit," I sigh. "What about the children?" I ask Thorne.

"What children?" Cam asks.

I close my eyes, not sure how to explain who the children are without an hour-long soliloquy. "Three immortal children were taken by Eudora, the Goddess of the Sea, and her demigod daughter, Marnie. The children are our priority right now. We'll keep the grimoire safe until we find them, then worry about Sable."

"Elsbeth. If Sable gets her hands on the spell contained in that book, the immortal children will be no more. Neither will any of you. At least the way that you know. One thing I've learned through old age is that sometimes priorities change." Phyllis's tone turns less jovial.

"I can't abandon them." I fight the tears threatening to fall.

"No one is asking you to abandon them. But in order to win the war and save them, this is a battle that must be fought first." Phyllis's words hit home. I know she's right, but the thought of Alex, Autumn, and Everly suffering at the hands of that monster for one more day is nearly more than I can take.

"She's right, acushla."

"For what it's worth, I agree." Cam props his arms on his hips, flexing his thick biceps in the process.

I turn toward the older witch. "What do we need to do?"

"It's easy." She smiles. "With the combination of your powers and the grimoire, you stand a chance."

"Stand a chance? You mean, even with our abilities and being vampires, we merely stand a *chance* against this woman?"

"Eh, I'd say fifty-fifty." The look on Phyllis's face tells me she thinks these are good odds.

"That's half," Cam adds. "I'll take that."

"Aye," Thorne adds, wrapping his long fingers through mine.

"How do we find her?"

"We won't have to search. She found you once, she'll find you again. Especially now that she knows you have the book." Phyllis moves toward the door. "If you don't mind, I'd like to place some protection around the home and property." She exits through the foyer, leaving Thorne and me alone with the oversized lycanthrope.

"Charleston is way more exciting than New Orleans." Cam smiles as he speaks. "Oh, I hope that didn't offend anyone."

"No offense taken. Seems you're correct." Thorne bends down, kissing me on the forehead. "I'm going to see if I can help."

Cam doesn't respond as he follows Thorne outside. Thoughts of the children flash through my mind. I know Phyllis is right. To save them, we have to stop Sable first. I collapse onto the couch behind me, still clutching the grimoire. For the first time in a while, I allow a dark thought into my mind. Maybe I should've let Kragen kill me...

a heritage complete

WHILE THORNE, Cam, and Phyllis work on the wards outside the house, I flip through the grimoire and work on clearing my mind of the darkness that's fighting to take over. For the first time since receiving the book, I read through a few of the spells.

Most seem relatively simple. Just a few ingredients, a few words, and poof—magic, or at least that's what I'm assuming. Out of the thirty or so pages in the grimoire, half of them are nothing but off-white parchment paper. "What's on this page?" I absentmindedly whisper at the empty page in my hand. With my words, letters begin to appear. *Protection,* the title reads at the top. "What the hell was that?" As quickly as they appeared, the words disappear. Was that my imagination?

Carrying the book outside, I find Thorne and Cam following Phyllis around the yard like lost sheep. Both have confused looks on their faces and remind me of children following a parent around at the store rather than the fierce paranormal creatures they are.

"Phyllis? I have a question." I hold the book in front of me. "On one of the blank pages, a spell appeared, then disappeared."

"Show me."

I flip the book to the blank page. "It was right here. It said protection at the top."

Phyllis laughs. "Seems that even from the grave, Aaron is trying to help."

"You think he was trying to help protect us?" I can't hide the *what-the-hell* look on my face.

"Elsbeth, I can't begin to explain the way magic works to someone who hasn't been around it their entire life. Hell, I don't even understand how it works sometimes. I guess that's why the universe named it magic—that's exactly what it is." She gently lays her hand on top of mine. "You're going to have to take my word for it. Aaron will send the spell when it's needed."

"He's dead."

"Yes, Aaron's dead, but his magic isn't. The grimoire holds bits and pieces of his magic, which means it holds pieces of him."

I stare at the woman in front of me. "Thank you, Phyllis."

"You're welcome, my dear." She turns behind her, staring at her vampire and lycanthrope shadows.

"Think you can help me find a *job* for these two?" She winks with her words.

"I think I can help you with that." I turn toward the duo. I'm not sure when we adopted Cam, but it seems he's not leaving. "I could use some help with some defensive fighting moves. Would you guys be willing to help?"

"Of course, acushla," Thorne answers first, moving to my side.

"Cam? It would be nice to see how things are done from a wolf's perspective," I lie.

"Oh, sure. I've never really been in a true *fight*, but I grew up with five older brothers. I can hold my own."

"Holy cannoli. Five older brothers?" Ms. Phyllis asks. "Your poor mother. Give her a hug for me."

Cam smiles, lifting one side of his mouth higher than the other. "I would, but she's gone. She was killed when I was still a teenager. It's a long story."

"I'm sorry, Cameron." Phyllis's voice is soft. "I didn't mean to bring up something negative."

"You didn't. It was a long time ago. She was a wonderful woman, and I got to spend sixteen years with her. When my dad passed, my oldest brother became the alpha and took over the pack."

"For what it's worth, I've met many lycan throughout my lifetime. Your energy is some of the warmest I've felt."

"Thank you, Ms. Phyllis. But I'm supposed to terrify people around me, not be warm and fuzzy. I'm a lycanthrope." He claws his bare hand in the air with a soft "roar," making the elderly witch laugh. His energy is relaxed and easy, reminding me of Luna.

Phyllis clutches her chest teasingly. "Oh, that was terrifying. How could I have been so wrong about you?"

"Pfft." He scoffs, following Thorne and me away from the working witch. "I like her," he announces once we're out of earshot.

"Yeah, me, too," I agree.

"I'm guessing Phyllis asked you to entertain us?" Thorne asks, making me smile.

"Aye. She did." The three of us stop underneath the canopy of a large shade tree. I turn toward Cam, hoping to change the subject. "What's it like having five older brothers? I was the oldest in my family. I'm curious to hear the other side."

He laughs. "There was never a dull moment growing up. I was the smallest, which meant I had to learn to fight early."

"You would fight each other?" Thorne asks.

"Yeah. We used to wolf out and try to kill each other over the dumbest things."

Thorne and I stare at the lycanthrope. "Really?"

Cam shrugs. "Yeah. It was fun." He laughs deeply. "There was this one time that my brother Colby nearly killed me. I was in the hospital for weeks after that fight. That's when Dad stopped allowing us to roughhouse."

"That was fun for you?" I ask, watching him reminisce over a near-death experience.

"Of course."

"Do you know anything about fighting witches?" Thorne redirects our conversation.

Cam clears his throat. "Even though I'm tasked with keeping the covens in line, today was my first experience with fighting an actual witch. Most are docile and follow the rules."

"So, none of us really knows what we're up against." I lean against the trunk of a large live oak tree.

"It's a battle that can't be won with physical strength. We have to use magic." Thorne's right. This isn't going to be a battle of who's the strongest. It's going to be a battle of whose magic is the most powerful.

"I'm afraid all I can provide is brute force," Cam says, flexing his biceps in an awkward goofball way, providing the comic relief we need.

"Brute force is helpful, too," I announce, moving in front of the lycanthrope. "Don't take offense to what I'm about to do."

"What..." is the only word Cam gets out as I move vampire speed behind him, wrapping my arms and legs around his torso and bringing my fangs to his throat.

"Your brute force needs work," I tease, clinging to his back.

"Shit. I wasn't ready. I...I didn't realize we were going all out." Cam's heart rate has picked up significantly, sending the blood flowing through his veins faster. The temptation to drink is strong.

"Don't," Thorne warns, sensing my desire.

Before I have time to think, the man I'm clinging to shifts into wolf form, throwing me to the ground. The wolf turns toward me, snarling a warning. *"What the hell was that?"* screams through my mind.

"Cam?"

"Yeah, it's me." His voice is deep and out of breath.

"How can I hear you and you hear me?"

"Well, this is an interesting development," Thorne's familiar brogue joins the conversation.

"Can you hear our thoughts in human form?" I ask out loud.

The wolf shakes his head dramatically, leaving a path of slobber along the way. *"I don't think so. This is the first time."* Cam sits on his hind legs, staring into my eyes. *"Does this mean I have some sort of witch's blood?"*

"Maybe a little. I'm of the belief that we all have a little magic inside us," Phyllis says from a few feet behind. She claps her hands loudly. "What a fun day."

"You can hear us, too?"

She shrugs. "I don't think I heard everything, but I definitely heard that. Cam was shouting through his mind, and it was as clear as day."

"Can all witches hear thoughts?" Thorne asks.

"No," she answers quickly. "I've known a few others in my lifetime, but only aware of one at the moment."

"Who?" Cam asks, now back in human form and standing naked without a care in the world.

"Sable." Phyllis looks Cam up and down, pausing in a certain area. "Hmm, I've always wondered what sort of package a man of your size would have." She crosses her arms over her chest. "I'm pleasantly surprised." For the first time since meeting him, Cam seems to gain a bit of modesty. Large hands move in front of his groin, blocking him from our eyes.

Phyllis's laugh echoes off the side of the house. "Don't cover up on my behalf. I'm too old for such things. But," she pauses, "looking never hurt anyone."

Cam's ears burn red as he turns toward the house, covering his bare ass with his other hand. "There are clothes upstairs that should fit," Thorne calls after him.

The moment the door closes, the three of us burst into the sort of laughter that brings tears to your eyes. "Oh, my word. I needed that," Phyllis announces.

"What? Cam naked or the laugh?" I ask.

She shrugs. "Both. Ok, it's training time," she announces with a loud clap, looking between the two of us. "Are you ready?"

"Yes," we answer in unison.

"Would you mind grabbing a few things from the house, Thorne?" she asks the vampire at my side.

"Of course."

"I was hoping you'd say that. We need a candle and salt." Thorne disappears and reappears before Phyllis has time to turn around. "That was quick," she laughs, taking the items.

I watch as she squats to the ground. "Join me." She pats the grass next to her. Thorne and I follow instructions, sitting on either side of her. "Elsie, let's start with you. Place this candle wherever you want."

Taking the pink taper candle from her hand, I put it a few feet in front of my knees, making sure it's standing straight and tall.

"Now, make a small circle around it using the salt."

I take the salt and begin pinching small amounts around the candle. "This seems weird," I whisper.

Phyllis laughs. "It may seem that way, but it's going to ground you."

"Ground me?"

"Yes, ground you. It will help build confidence and center your energy. Now, light the wick and focus on the flame while you repeat after me."

"Burn," I whisper, bringing the wick to life.

"Earth below, flame bright, calm my mind, grant me sight," Phyllis says, and I echo. "Let my spirit grounded be, centered, calm, and wild, yet free." I echo the words, feeling a strange peace enter my body. "Now, close your eyes, take a deep breath, and let the energy settle within you."

I follow instructions, allowing the calm to spread from the top of my head through my body until it exits my feet. I open my eyes to the warm smiles of both of my companions. "Did it work?" I ask, not sure if anything happened.

"How do you feel?" Phyllis asks.

I shrug. "I don't know. Relaxed?"

"Then it worked. Snuff out the candle, and Thorne will do the same." I watch as Thorne lights the candle and repeats the actions and words. The sense of calm I feel is different. The energy that fills the world around me gives me a sense of tranquility for the first time in a while.

"How do you feel?" Phyllis asks Thorne.

"Really good," he answers. "I feel like I've slept for several days."

Phyllis laughs. "I thought vampires didn't sleep."

"We don't," he answers, flopping backward on the grass. "Are all spells this easy?"

"No. That was a beginner spell." She slowly stands, grunting a few times along the way. "You both did well. I could feel the energy flowing through you." Phyllis moves to take a step, and her knee gives out. Thorne is at her side before she falls, keeping her off the ground. "Oh, goodness." She laughs. "Between protecting the house and that spell, I'm a little tired."

"We have plenty of space," I interrupt, moving to her side. "Thorne can take you to a room where you can rest."

"That would be perfect. Thank you." I watch the two of them slowly make their way into the house just as Cam exits. Phyllis has enough energy left to swat the lycanthrope on the ass on her way past. His eyes grow twice their size as he mouths the words, *"Help me."*

"What's going on?" he asks, moving to my side.

"Phyllis overdid it a little. Thorne's taking her to lie down."

"She's dying." Cam's words are simple and straightforward.

"What?" I turn toward him. "What are you talking about?"

"Phyllis. She's dying."

"Are you speaking metaphorically or literally?"

Cam sighs. "Phyllis is, or rather was, the protector of the grimoire, as her ancestors have done before her. Now that you are here and have the grimoire, her lineage is complete."

I turn, facing the open window of the room Thorne took her to. "How long does she have?"

"I don't know. I've only read about this sort of thing, but from what I've read, it varies. A few years, a few months, a few days..."

"A few days?" Guilt fills me. "Can I do something to change it?"

"I don't know," he answers honestly, staring into the same window I am.

"Does she know?"

"Yes. The moment she gave you access to the grimoire, the process began."

"That's simply unacceptable," I retort, heading into the house and leaving Cam alone in the backyard.

Racing up the stairs and opening the door to her room, I find Thorne helping Phyllis get into bed. "Elsie? Do you mind me calling you Elsie?"

"No." I smile. "It's been my nickname since I was a kid."

Phyllis laughs softly. "Okay, good. I have to ask. Were you worried I was going to take advantage of Thorne up here all alone?"

I stare at the wide plank floorboard in front of me, not sure what to say. I direct my thoughts toward the older witch. *So, you're going to die? Is that the truth?*

"Yes, I am. It's true," she answers, reading my mind.

"What are we talking about?" Thorne asks as he covers her legs with a throw blanket from the foot of the bed.

"It seems Elsie has just discovered my demise." She yawns widely as she speaks. Wrinkled hands smooth the blanket covering her.

"Your demise?" Thorne looks between us. "Can someone explain, please?"

I sigh before answering. "Now that Phyllis has given me Aaron's grimoire, her life's mission is completed, meaning...meaning she's dying."

Thorne whips his head toward the elder witch. "Dying? Why?"

"Just as Elsie explained. My ancestors were tasked with guarding and protecting the grimoire. Now that our job is complete, I'm not needed."

"I don't want it," I interrupt. "You can take it back."

"It's not that easy, dear. You are the rightful heir to the grimoire. You can't just simply return it like a shirt that's too small."

"There has to be another way," Thorne adds.

Phyllis smiles, lifting one side of her mouth higher than the other. "Look at you two. You're vampires, for goddess's sake. You're supposed to be terrifying, heartless, and cruel...the adjectives go on and on. Instead, you're sad about an old witch dying. I've lived my life. I've completed my task. I'm happy. Besides, I'm just tired today. I'm not dying today or even next week. I'll be here as long as I'm needed."

"But you got tired and needed to lie down," I retort.

"Because I'm old and worked all day at the library dealing with shitheads who don't know how to reshelve a damn book. Using my energy wore me down slightly, but not any more than usual." She claps her hands loudly. "Now, if you'll excuse me, I'm going to take a nap and dream about a hot lycanthrope." She wiggles her eyebrows, dismissing us with her words.

family trees

I SPEND the next few hours reading through each spell in the grimoire, hoping to commit at least a few of them to memory. To be honest, I don't know how witches are able to keep the spells separated. After a while, the words and spells all seem to run together.

Thorne's been in the room with me but glued to a laptop the entire time. I haven't asked what he's researching, and he hasn't volunteered any information.

Cam's lycan energy is still nearby, but I have no idea what he's doing. Do I care? No. However, from what I've learned about the lycanthrope, it could be anything.

Thorne closes the laptop and takes a deep breath. "I can't find any information on her."

"Who?"

"Serafina." He slides the computer to the couch next

to him and stretches his long legs. I thought maybe there'd be something about her ancestry online, but I haven't found any helpful information. I can't even find evidence of her birth."

"You remember how it was in the 17th century in Scotland. Unless she was born to a noble family, her birth may not have even been recorded."

"Aye, but there's nothing on her death, either. I'm assuming she died here in Charleston. It's like she never existed."

Thorne runs his hands through his hair, making it stand on end. "Who never existed?" Cam asks, entering the room. "Sorry, I didn't mean to be eavesdropping. I just heard the last part."

"Serafina," Thorne answers.

"Where were you looking?" Cam asks. "Online?"

"Aye. There's nothing."

"That's because you need to look in the right places. Most communities, vampire," Cam motions toward Thorne and me, "lycan," he touches his chest, "and witches, don't allow information like that to be written down for just anyone to see."

"Is there a secret library somewhere?" I ask, half joking, half serious.

Cam props his hands on his hips. "Of course." The tone of his voice is almost comedic in its intention. "How did you not know that?"

Thorne and I share a look, neither of us sure how to

answer. "Maybe it's too secretive," Thorne answers, making me laugh.

"As far as I know, every city with a large population of paranormal people has one." Cam sits on an over-stuffed chair.

"Can you take us there?" I ask the giant lycanthrope.

He shrugs. "If I knew where it was, yeah."

"Seriously?"

Cam holds his hands up. "In my defense, you didn't ask if I knew where it was, just if there was one."

I send a burst of energy into Cam, not enough to hurt him, just enough to give him a tiny shock. I'm rewarded when he leaps from the chair, holding his backside. "What the hell was that?"

"What?" I play dumb.

"Something bit my ass." I watch in silence as he pulls the cushion from the chair, searching for the invisible creature.

"I feel like a new woman," Phyllis says, stopping on the bottom step and watching the spectacle in front of her. "What's going on here?"

"Something bit Cam's ass," I answer, still refusing to divulge my secret.

"I'd like to bite—"

"Phyllis," Thorne interrupts with perfect timing. "Do you happen to know if there's a place where we could study the ancestry of witches, lycan, and vampires in Charleston? A library, perhaps. A *hidden* library."

"I don't know where the library is at the moment."

"Does it move?" I ask, confused.

"Yes," she answers simply. "It's moved for its own protection."

"How do we find out where it is?" Cam asks, still rubbing his butt cheek.

Phyllis looks each of us in the eye. "It's one of our coven's most guarded secrets. Like my ancestors were tasked with the protection of Aaron's grimoire, there is a family tasked with the protection of the library. They're the ones responsible for its whereabouts and the only ones who know where it is."

"Dumb question," Cam interrupts. "If no one knows where it is, how do people add their information?"

"Not a dumb question, my wolf friend. There's a ritual, a guard, and a whole process that I can't divulge." Phyllis winks with her words.

"Does anyone know who the family is?" Thorne asks.

"No one knows. Well, most don't." Phyllis smiles crookedly. "Lucky for you, I'm not most."

"Can you take us there?" I ask.

"There are secrets in those records that have remained secrets for centuries. As far as I know, no witch, lycan, or vampire has been given access to them other than the family assigned to protect them. What are you looking for?"

"Serafina," Thorne answers. "If she's from Scotland, maybe our families knew each other. I don't know what I'm looking for, but something tells me I need to look."

Phyllis stares into Thorne's soft blue eyes for a moment before answering. "Okay. I'll contact the guardian." She walks outside, pulling a cell phone from her back pocket.

"What do you think you'll find?" Cam asks.

"I have no idea."

The door opens, revealing the elderly witch. "Okay," she answers. "There's one condition."

"What is it?" I ask.

"Cam has to sit in the front seat with me on the drive over."

I can't hide the smile covering my face. Whether Phyllis really has the hots for Cam or just enjoys making him uncomfortable, I'm here for it.

Ten minutes later, we're pulling away from our Charleston home in the backseat of Phyllis's SUV. Cam is in the front seat, leaving plenty of room between him and our driver. Our drive is short and takes us to a small house on the riverfront a few miles away. "This is it," Phyllis announces, sliding out of her vehicle.

"The records are here?" Cam asks. "This looks like an ordinary house."

"That's the point."

Energy floods me. It's an energy I've become familiar with over the past months. "Do you feel that?" I ask Thorne.

"Aye. Lycan. Cam, do you recognize who is here?"

Cam turns his head toward us. "No. It's not someone I've met before, and the energy feels... strange."

"Get your asses out of the truck. She's waiting," Phyllis reprimands.

The three of us reluctantly follow the witch to the front door. She knocks in a sequence of three short knocks, followed by a fist hit.

"Is that a secret knock?" Cam whispers.

"No."

The door opens, revealing a woman who appears to be not much older than me. Her chestnut-colored hair, rich with tones of brown and red, flows in natural waves, framing her angular face. Piercing green eyes shine bright against her dark complexion, giving her incomparable beauty.

"Hello, witch." She smiles at Phyllis before looking at Thorne and me. "Hello, bloodsuckers." She turns to Cam. "Hello, wolf."

"Um, hi." Cam waves awkwardly. "I'm Cameron... St. James. I mean, Cam."

"Nice to meet you, Cam. My name is Nyssa Jamison." She turns back to Thorne and me. "You're Captain Hawthorne Rex, and you're," she looks me in the eyes, sniffing the air around me, "you're Elsbeth Abernathy."

"I am," I answer. "How do you know us?"

"I've done quite a bit of research over the years."

Cam leans against the side of the house, propping

an arm and a foot. "I've done research through the years." He clears his throat.

"Is that so?" Nyssa asks with a smile. "Won't you all come in?" She steps aside, leaving room for the four of us to enter.

Thorne places a hand on Phyllis's back, ushering her into the home, followed by me. The first thing I notice is the smell of food. Normally, smelling human food disgusts me, but this smells nothing short of amazing.

"Something smells like a piece of heaven," Phyllis announces, taking the words from my mouth.

"I was making some soup," Nyssa answers. "Would you care for any?"

"I would." Cam raises his hand. "Please." He clears his throat for the second time.

"That would be perfect," Phyllis answers. "The thing about hanging out with vampires is they're not interested in food."

Nyssa excuses herself and returns moments later with two heaping bowls of soup topped with a thick piece of what looks like cornbread. "What brings you to me today?" she asks, setting the bowls in front of Cam and Phyllis.

"I'm looking for information on a witch named Serafina," Thorne answers. "She was originally from Scotland..."

"I know who Serafina is. Why are you searching for information on her?"

"We're from the same time period and the same country. I'm curious if there's a possibility my family might have known hers or was related somehow. To be honest, I don't know what I'm looking for. A connection, maybe."

Nyssa sits on a chair in the corner of the room, facing the rest of us. "Please, have a seat." She motions to a large couch opposite her. Cam and Phyllis immediately begin working on their soup while Thorne and I sit between them.

"This is the best soup I've ever eaten," Cam announces, bringing the edge of the bowl to his lips and draining it in one gulp.

"Thank you," Nyssa answers with a smile. She turns her attention back to Thorne. "Why don't you tell me the real reason you're looking for information on Serafina?"

"I'm not sure what you mean," he answers.

"I feel the power inside you, Captain. There's more than just a vampire in there." She averts her eyes toward me. "Both of you."

"Aye."

"What are you really looking for?" Nyssa asks again.

"Serafina," Thorne repeats.

"You're looking for more than a name listed, aren't you?"

"*What's she talking about?*" I ask through our connection.

"Aye," he answers the lycanthrope, ignoring me.

"Thorne?"

"You're wondering if there's a possibility you could be related." Nyssa's words are a statement, not a question.

"Aye," Thorne whispers.

Nyssa slides forward in her chair. "What good would it do to know if you are or are not related?"

"It would answer..." he pauses, not finishing.

"Where your power comes from," Nyssa finishes his statement.

"Aye."

The lycanthrope slides out of her seat, disappearing into another room. "She's intense," Phyllis whispers just before Nyssa returns, carrying a large book. She sets it on the table at Thorne's knees, opening it to a page titled "Rex." Below the name is a perfectly drawn family crest and tree.

"I believe you'll find the information you seek here." Thorne slides forward, drawing the book closer. "You should know that the names in that book come from powerful magic."

Thorne slowly traces his family name and crest. *"Would you like some privacy?"* I ask through our connection.

"No," he answers out loud.

"You'll find your name further down," Nyssa says, watching him read through the names.

Thorne slowly rubs his fingers along the perfect script until landing on a familiar name. The name of the captain who brought my family to America. "Hawthorne Finley," he reads. He traces the lines that connect to his siblings. "Mary Arabella and Joseph Arley. I was the oldest." Thorne has never spoken of his family. Hearing their names for the first time sends a chill down my spine.

"Follow that line further," Nyssa encourages.

Pulling the book closer, Thorne traces his fingers against a long-ago erased line. Even with vampire vision, the name is barely visible. "Serafina Elizabeth," I whisper. "Could it be?"

Nyssa smiles. "Yes. Serafina was your half-sister. Your father had a short *fling* with the nursemaid. You and Serafina share the same blood."

"Well, shit," Phyllis says from his other side. "That explains your power."

"How did you know about her name being erased?" I ask our lycanthrope host.

"It's my job to know, as it has been for those before me. I am a lycanthrope, yes, but my mother was descended from a powerful line of witches. Witches charged with keeping these records safe." Nyssa shrugs. "My mother enjoyed the nightlife of New Orleans a little too much when she was younger. Hence, my sperm donor is like you, Cameron St. James— lycan." Cam doesn't respond. Awkwardness flows from him as he squirms in his seat.

"If Serafina is my half-sister, what does that mean?"

"It means you may be the only one capable of

defeating Sable," Nyssa answers with a smirk covering her face.

"You mean Sable," I interrupt. "Serafina is dead."

Nyssa's laugh fills the room. "There is no Sable. The two are one and the same. The woman you know as Sable is, in fact, Serafina."

"Fuck," Phyllis whispers.

unimaginable power

"HOW IS it possible for Serafina to still be alive?" Thorne asks our lycanthrope host. "She's just a witch." Phyllis sighs loudly at his words. "No offense intended, Ms. Phyllis. It's just that she's not immortal...is she?"

"Witches are not immortal, no," Nyssa answers. "Your naivety is amusing, though. There are other ways for someone to live past their years."

"A spell?" Phyllis acknowledges the elephant in the room.

"Yes."

"You should do that, Phyllis," Cam adds to the conversation.

"It's against the rules," Nyssa interrupts.

"Rules?" I ask. "Who determines the rules?"

"The High Coven," Phyllis answers. "They're a group of elite witches, mostly coven leaders from major cities around the world."

"Like the Vampire Council," Thorne says through my mind.

"There's no need to use telepathy, Mr. Rex. You are surrounded by people who can hear with means other than our ears."

"Speak for yourself," Cam adds.

"I believe you have that ability, too," Nyssa says.

"Only in wolf form."

Nyssa smiles. "I'd like to see your wolf form."

Cam returns the smile. "I'd like to see yours."

Nyssa turns her attention back to Thorne. "Yes, like the Vampire Council. The High Coven assures the safety of our craft and keeps those who wish to distort our abilities at bay."

"How the hell has Serafina snuck through?" I huff.

"Serafina is very powerful. No doubt a spell has protected her until now."

I stand, moving toward a large granite fireplace. "Why is staying young against the rules? As long as she's not hurting anyone, what does it matter?" Thorne glances at me.

Nyssa stands, moving to the opposite wall and faces me. "Magic strongly emphasizes balance with nature and the natural order of life and death. A spell that extends life is a violation of that belief. A prolonged life could result in an accumulation of magical residue that can corrupt the witch and her community over time."

"In other words, it's a disruption of the natural balance of things," Phyllis adds.

"Aren't vampires a disruption of the natural balance?" I ask the two witches. "We don't die."

"No," Nyssa answers simply. "The mere fact that you are a vampire is the balance. You died to become what you are. A death for a life." I've never thought about my life that way. She's right. I died to become the killer I am. Irony at its finest.

"What would happen if the High Coven were to discover Serafina and the spell keeping her alive?" Cam asks.

"To be honest, I don't know."

"If you knew Serafina was still alive and using a spell to stay young, why haven't you contacted them?" I ask the obvious question.

Nyssa smiles before answering. "As the caretaker of the records, I am privy to information that no one else has access to, even the High Coven. As a witch, I am expected to follow the rules of my heritage. As care-taker, I am tasked with keeping secrets. Some of those secrets are small, some larger." Nyssa slides her hands into the pockets of her skin-tight jeans. "I am bound by my heritage and promise. I cannot share information unless specifically asked."

"You shared it with us," Thorne takes the words out of my mouth.

"I shared your heritage and sister with you. Phyllis shared the spell."

Kragen's words come to mind. *Semantics.* Nyssa smiles, obviously reading my thoughts.

"The High Coven must find out," Phyllis says, standing from the couch. "It's my responsibility to let them know."

"Then what?" Cam asks.

"Then we fight," Phyllis answers.

"If you'd allow, I'd like to join you. I believe I offer a special set of abilities that could be useful in defeating Serafina." Nyssa moves to Cam's side.

"Who will guard the records?" Phyllis asks.

"They are well guarded. I'm allowed to leave every once in a while. This sounds like just the sort of adventure I need." She motions to the lavishly decorated living area. "These walls tend to close in on themselves after a while."

Cam stands. "If something happens to you, who will take over here?"

"There are safety measures in place," she answers, not giving details. Nyssa looks at each of us. "Are we ready?"

"Now?" Thorne asks. "We don't have a plan."

"I believe the first part of the plan needs to be to discover Serafina's purpose."

"We know what she wants," I answer. I make eye contact with Phyllis, who nods, telling me to trust Nyssa. "She wants Aaron Abernathy's grimoire."

Nyssa wrinkles her forehead. "I don't have that book in my library."

"No, you don't. I do," I answer.

"How?" Nyssa looks between Phyllis and me. "I was

led to believe that his grimoire was destroyed centuries ago.

"My ancestors kept it safe."

Nyssa smiles, crossing her arms at her chest. "You had Aaron Abernathy's grimoire this entire time?"

"Well, my ancestors did originally, then me. But yes, I've held it for the past fifty years."

"What does she want with Aaron's grimoire?" Nyssa asks me.

"Inside the grimoire is a spell that Serafina wants." I don't feel comfortable sharing what the spell does with a woman I've just met.

"What kind of spell would Serafina spend centuries chasing after?" Nyssa asks.

"One that was worth hiding," Phyllis answers without answering.

"I feel the need to ask. Why do we have to kill Serafina?" Cam asks everyone in the room. "If Phyllis contacts the High Coven, isn't it their job to punish her or whatever the hell they do?"

"If Serafina gets her hands on that spell, the High Coven won't stand a chance," Thorne answers, reminding me of the severity of the binding spell.

"This is getting more interesting by the minute," Nyssa says.

"What do you sense in me?" Thorne asks, changing the subject.

"Great power," Nyssa answers. "I've felt power like

yours before, but only on rare occasions, and honestly, your power feels stronger."

"I don't know how to use it," he admits. "I'm going to be useless without that knowledge."

"The power is there, even if you can't feel it." Nyssa leaves the room, exiting the same way as earlier. She returns moments later, carrying a book that looks similar to Aaron's. "Something ancient will help draw your magic out."

Nyssa flips pages in the large book. "Here. Blood and earth. Blood, to open his spirit, and earth to keep him grounded."

"He'll need a guide," Phyllis adds. "One of us will be his anchor while the other will act as a bridge between Thorne and the magic."

"Agreed. We need to be careful. Ancient magic doesn't like to be contained," Nyssa says.

"I'll gather the earth." Phyllis takes her empty soup bowl and exits the front door.

"I'll be right back," Nyssa says, leaving the three of us alone.

Cam makes eye contact with me. "Anyone else nervous?" His voice is no louder than a whisper.

Thorne doesn't respond, but his body language tells me his answer is yes. Nyssa is the first one back. She's holding a small crystal. "This is smoky quartz. It will anchor your energy."

"I've got dirt," Phyllis says, coming through the door.

"Join us," Nyssa says as she and Phyllis stand in the middle of the room. Thorne moves slowly in front of them. She hands him the crystal. "Keep this in your hand, and don't let go no matter what you feel." Thorne nods.

Phyllis takes a small handful of dirt, pressing it into his forehead and heart. "From earth, you are bound."

Nyssa pulls a dagger from her belt buckle, pressing it into her wrist. The smell of copper fills the room as she cuts her palm. "From blood, you are opened." She wipes blood on top of Phyllis's dirt before placing her wrist in front of Thorne's mouth. "Drink, vampire."

"No," he refuses.

"You must," she continues.

Thorne sighs before wrapping his free hand around her wrist. "Elsie?"

"I've got you," I reassure him. I know he's asking me to keep him from taking too much.

"Are you sure about this?" he asks the lycanthrope in front of him. She nods, giving him permission. Thorne latches onto her wrist and moans as he begins to drink. The earth on his forehead and chest begins to glow with unsourced light, turning the same color as the crystal held tightly in his hand.

He releases Nyssa's wrists with a loud gasp. His bright eyes flash green as the energy in the room becomes heavier than before. Thorne stands perfectly still as power flows into and through him. Nyssa stumbles backward with Thorne's release. Cam wraps an arm around her, keeping her upright. "It is done," she says breathlessly.

"Thorne?" I don't know whether to wrap my arms around his waist or move out of his way. "Are you okay?"

"Aye," he answers. "I think so."

"How do you feel?" Cam asks.

"Different, but the same, if that makes sense."

"The power of your ancestors has been awakened," Phyllis says, sitting on the chair beside her.

"What do I do with it?" Thorne asks.

"You use it to defeat your half-sister," Phyllis answers simply. "I thought that was a given."

"Are you alright?" he asks Nyssa.

She sucks in a deep breath. "I will be. The combination of blood loss and the use of my powers was more than I was ready for. I don't get to use my powers as much as I should. Give me a few minutes." She pulls away from Cam's side, still wobbly on her feet. Cam keeps a hand protectively on her back.

"It's clear that no one is ready to do battle at this minute. Why don't Thorne and I take Phyllis back to the house to rest? Cam, stay with Nyssa until her energy returns, then you can join us." I'm not sure when I turned into the boss, but I roll with it.

"Okay," Cam answers, leading Nyssa to the couch.

I wrap my arm around Phyllis, helping her to stand, and slowly move toward her truck. "I'll drive if you're okay with that."

"I think that's for the best," Phyllis answers, handing me a set of keys. "Phew, I feel like I've had one or twenty too many drinks." Thorne helps her into the back seat before climbing in beside her and strapping her safely under the seat belt.

It doesn't take long to get back to the house. Pulling the SUV into the driveway, I move it as far away from the street as possible. "She's asleep," Thorne says, lifting her from the leather seat. Cradling her to his chest, he carries her inside and straight upstairs to the room where she rested earlier.

"Are you okay?" I repeat as he joins me in the dining room.

"Why do you keep asking me if I'm okay? I'm fine."

I stare at the man I've loved for three centuries, not sure how to respond. Since reconnecting, he's never used that tone of voice with me. "I'm sorry. I'm just worried about you."

"I'm fine, Elsie." He sits heavily on a dining chair, propping his boots on the antique mahogany table. "We need a plan."

"Yeah, we do. It's probably better to wait for Cam and Nyssa to get here and Phyllis to wake up before we come up with something set in stone." Thorne's energy feels—strange.

"You don't think I can come up with a plan on my own?"

What the hell? Thorne has turned into a narcissistic

asshole in less than an hour. "That's not what I'm saying. Four heads are better than one."

Thorne stares at the glass cabinet full of priceless porcelain. A large plate lifts off the cabinet and crashes to the ground, making me jump. Thorne laughs at my response. "You're a vampire, and a falling plate scared you?"

Moving to the table, I knock his long legs to the floor. "Enough. What the hell is wrong with you?"

"I don't know what you're talking about."

"This. You're not acting like yourself. You're being an asshole."

"Maybe this is the real me. After all, I am a vampire. Something I did to find *you*." He scoffs, standing to his feet. "I'm so glad I did that."

"Hawthorne Finley," I reprimand. "I didn't ask you to become a vampire for me. I sacrificed myself to save you. To save everyone on board your ship. You decided to become what you are. Don't put that on me."

He stomps off, heading to the refrigerator. The sound of bottles rattling grabs my attention. "All we have is this shit." The door slams, and he returns, holding a full bottle. "I hate this fake ass shit."

"Thorne, you're scaring me."

"What's the matter? Do I remind you of your pirate?" He takes a huge gulp of goat blood. His words are too much.

"How dare you compare yourself to Kragen?"

"Maybe Kragen was right. Maybe humans are

nothing more than food." He throws the empty bottle across the room.

The door opens just as the bottle shatters against the wall next to it. Cam and Nyssa are standing in the doorframe with confused looks on their faces. "What's going on?" Cam asks.

"Nothing more than I'm tired of fake blood," Thorne answers.

"I get that." Cam closes the door behind the lycan. "We all get tired of shit every once in a while."

"Thorne isn't acting like himself," I announce. Thorne props his hands on his hips and mimics my words.

"I can see that," Cam answers. "What's going on, man?"

"I've had an awakening," Thorne answers.

"What kind of awakening?" Nyssa asks.

"I'm leaving," he announces.

"Where are you going?" I ask, crossing my arms in front of my chest.

"Out. I'm hungry." Thorne moves faster than even my eyes can track and is out the door in a heartbeat.

The three of us stare at the still-open front door. "What the hell was that?" Cam asks. "Is that normal?"

"I don't know. This is a first for me," Nyssa answers.

"I'm going to follow him," Cam says, running out the door.

Nyssa and I stare awkwardly at each other for a few minutes before she speaks. "My guess is he's feeling emotions and having thoughts that he's suppressed for centuries. The amount of magic that flowed through him was more than I've ever experienced from anyone before. It would be overwhelming for even the most experienced practitioner. I can't imagine what it was like for someone who's never felt the power before." She sits in the same seat Thorne was in earlier. "He's the only one like him in the world."

"Perfect."

what just happened?

SEVERAL HOURS PASS before Phyllis stumbles down the large staircase. Her normally perfectly coiffed hair is a disaster of frizz, reminding me of a rat's nest. "What's going on?" she asks, her words slightly slurred. "The energy is heavy and called to me."

"Thorne left," I answer truthfully.

"Is he not allowed to leave?" She scoffs.

"He wasn't acting like himself. He was angry and cruel. Definitely out of character for him. I'm the angry and cruel one. Thorne is levelheaded and wise."

"Where's the hot wolf?"

"He followed Thorne," Nyssa answers.

"So, what are we thinking?" Phyllis asks both of us.

"He's in trouble," I admit, allowing fear to take over my thoughts. I stand, moving toward the door. "I shouldn't have let him go."

"Elsie, stop," Phyllis interrupts. "Right now, he needs to be alone."

"He needs someone who understands," I retort.

"Do you understand? Because I don't." Nyssa stands, moving closer to the door. "I'm going to go out on a limb here and say, let him figure this out on his own. He's a grown-ass man."

Nyssa's words stop me in my tracks. She's right. Thorne is grown and perfectly capable of taking care of himself. My life trauma makes me feel like I have to fix everyone and everything. The front door opens, and Cam enters. "Where's Thorne?"

"He asked me to leave him alone."

"And you did? What if he does something dumb, or...or hurts someone?" I fight the tears forming in my eyes. Dammit, Elsie.

"I understand your frustration. He asked me to tell you to trust him and that he wasn't going to do anything stupid." Cam runs a hand through his already messy hair.

"Where was he when you left him?" My voice is no louder than a whisper.

"On the riverbank."

"Why do I feel so helpless?"

"You're not helpless, Elsie," Phyllis says, moving to my side. "Thorne will be okay. Everything he's known for the past three centuries has changed in one day. Give him a little grace to figure things out."

"He made a plate fall out of the cabinet earlier."

Phyllis looks at me and wrinkles her forehead. "Did he pick it up?"

"Not physically...with magic. He was angry. The plate lifted off the shelf and slammed to the floor." The witches share a look. "Is that not normal?" I ask.

"For some, yes. For others, no." Nyssa leans forward in her seat. "Not all witches control their power the same. Powers are as individualized as hair color."

"Nyssa is correct. It's also not customary for witches to share their methodology." Phyllis pulls a book from the overcrowded shelf. She holds the book in front of her, opening the pages wide. Like when we first met, the pages begin to flip as if someone were controlling them.

"An air witch," Nyssa says. "Nice."

"Air witch? What does that mean?"

"It means I can manipulate the wind, or in this case, a soft breeze that turns book pages. Thorne's manipulation of the plate would be a form of air magic."

"What form does Serafina hold?" Nyssa asks.

I shrug. "I have no idea."

"You've come in contact with her?"

"We have. She pretended to be Fran and Cam." I scoff at the memory.

Nyssa's eyes grow slightly. "Serafina pretended to be someone else? Did she accomplish this by changing her looks or changing the environment?"

I think back to our first encounter. "The environment. She made Thorne, and I think we flew to New Orleans and visited a new vampire."

Nyssa sits heavily on the couch. "Her power has grown."

I turn toward my house guest. "What do you mean? Do you know her other than through the books in your library?" Energy forms at my core.

"Yes," she answers. "Before you hit me with whatever you're brewing in there," she points at my core, "it's not what you think. She came to me looking for Aaron's grimoire."

"You just now thought to tell us this?" I spew. "It wasn't important before?"

"It was important, just not pertinent, and you didn't ask."

"What the hell does that mean?"

Nyssa stands, moving across the room. "She determined it was being held by our coven. She found out my ancestors were the ones in charge of the paranormal library and assumed his grimoire would be there." Nyssa looks at Phyllis. "She was wrong."

"When was this?" Phyllis asks.

"About six months ago."

"You think her power has grown in that time? How do you know?" Phyllis continues.

Nyssa inhales deeply. "Being a hybrid, my senses are heightened. It's allowed me to keep the library safe, and what allowed me to feel your power."

"Nonsense," Phyllis interrupts. "I felt their power. Lycan blood had nothing to do with that."

"It's stronger with me." Nyssa closes her eyes. "I know a person's ability just by feeling their energy." She turns toward me. "Like Phyllis, you're an elemental witch. You wield fire, along with an ability to listen to people's minds."

"Cam," she turns toward the stoic lycanthrope. "There is magic in your bloodline, but it's not very strong."

Cam shifts from foot to foot. "What kind of magic?"

"It feels bound in nature."

He laughs awkwardly. "I can control nature?"

"I wouldn't go that far. When you're in wolf form, you have more control than in human form. You have slight control over the trees."

"I do?"

"They bend and move at your will."

"Damn." He breathes. "When I was a kid, I felt like the trees spoke to me. My brothers told me I was dumb."

"They did. You are one with them," Nyssa continues. She turns back to me. "I felt Serafina's power. Her power was strong, yet I didn't feel the ability to alter reality."

"For someone as old as Serafina, I doubt she would be acquiring new abilities. My guess is she had knowledge of your ability and hid her power from you." Phyllis's words make sense.

"What's the purpose of all of this?" I ask the obvious question. "Yes, you said Aaron's grimoire holds a binding spell she was working on, but she's not dumb. If Serafina created a spell to bind paranormal creatures, Aaron taking the words away wouldn't take the spell away. She created it once; she can create it again. I'm guessing she's after something other than the binding spell."

Phyllis's eyes grow several sizes. "Where's the grimoire?"

"In my room," I answer, pointing upstairs.

"Would you get it, dear?"

I follow instructions, moving upstairs at vampire speed. The book is exactly where I left it, safely on top of the nightstand. I'm back downstairs in the blink of an eye.

"May I?" Phyllis asks, reaching for the book.

I reach out to hand it to her before something inside questions what I'm doing. My stomach ties into knots, something I haven't felt since becoming a vampire. I pull the book back to me. "Phyllis, what was the name of the girl who contacted me about the grimoire again? I seem to have forgotten her name."

"What are you talking about, Elsie?" the elder witch asks.

"You know. The girl who spent her summer cleaning up the basement. I can't seem to remember her name."

"Give me the book." She ignores my question.

"Phyllis?"

Nyssa moves closer to my side as the energy in the room shifts slightly. "What's going on?" Cam asks, feeling the shift.

"Don't be silly. I'm old and can't remember a damn intern's name. We've had so many over the years, they all run together."

"Take a guess," I encourage her, holding on to the book.

"Was it Emma, or was that last summer? Maybe it was Eloise." She takes a step closer. "Damn, I can't remember."

"What was her name, Phyllis?" I ask one last time.

In an instant, the elderly witch transforms into Serafina's beautiful face. "Damn, I thought I fooled you."

"Serafina," Nyssa whispers. "It was you the entire time."

"Not the entire time, just the last hour or so." She stretches her hands high above her head in a pretend stretch. "Phyllis had a nice nap."

"Where is she?" Cam asks.

"Don't worry, wolf. She's safe. I didn't hurt a hair on her little white head."

"How'd you get past the wards?" I ask.

"Pfff." She scoffs. "Wards are for weaklings. I'm not a weakling." She reaches her hand toward me once more. "Give me the book, Elsbeth."

"You already have the binding spell. What's in here that you want so badly?"

"Nothing that concerns you, bloodsucker."

"My brother's grimoire concerns me," I retort.

She stalks closer. "You never knew Aaron. I did." She stops inches from my face. "He was weak, like you."

"Aaron Abernathy was a powerful warlock," Nyssa argues.

Serafina smiles. "A warlock is only as strong as his ability. Like you, he lacked in that area. Although he was well-endowed and quite fun to play with. Did you know he used to cry after he came?"

"Shut up," I spew.

"You have no claim to his grimoire. It should be mine," she argues.

"You'll have to go through me first," I warn.

"That won't be an issue."

Instinctively, something takes over my energy, causing me to place my hand on the rune covering the front cover. "Pages bound and secrets kept, in silent shadows, tightly slept. None shall read nor pry inside until my voice calls to unbind." Words spew from my mouth as if they've been there all along.

"Bitch!" Serafina yells. "What did you do?"

"I don't know," I answer truthfully.

"You bound the book. Undo it."

"I...I don't know how." Holding the book tight to my chest, I make eye contact with Cam. He nods, letting me know he understands what I'm about to do. Seconds later, he transforms into a beautiful dark brown wolf. His shoulders are taller than Serafina's head.

"You don't scare me, wolf."

He growls, filling the house with sound. *"Go,"* he says into my mind. *"Don't let her get his book."*

One wolf turns into two as Nyssa transforms into Cam's solid black twin, nearly as tall as Cam. Piercing green eyes glare at Serafina as she scoffs at the lycan. I don't wait around to see what happens. I'm through the door and at the river's edge seconds later. *"Thorne!"* I call through our connection. *"Thorne!"*

"Here," a deep voice says behind me.

I turn, finding the man that I love. His hair is disheveled, and his clothes are torn. "What happened?" I ask.

"I...I fell into the river."

"You fell into the river?" I repeat, trying to make sense of his words. Vampires don't just fall.

"Aye. What's happened? Why do you have the grimoire?"

"Serafina's at the house. Cam and Nyssa are with her. She pretended to be Phyllis." Words fly out of my mouth in rapid succession. "We have to get out of here."

"Okay. Give me the book. I'm stronger than you and can keep it safe."

"You're not stronger than me," I argue. "I'm older and have lived off of human blood for centuries. I'm stronger. You know that."

Without responding, Thorne reaches his hand toward me, lacing his long fingers through mine. I follow him away from the river's edge. "We have to go, Thorne. She'll be here soon. The lycan won't be able to keep her from following me for much longer."

He turns, facing me. "Give me the grimoire, Elsie."

"Thorne?"

Bright blue eyes close, and the energy around us changes. Shadows form and pulsate with a silent tempo. Thorne begins chanting inaudible words as the wind picks up even more. I tighten my grip on the book, feeling its magic meld with mine. "Thorne," I beg. "You don't know what you're doing."

"I don't need to know," he whispers. "The magic knows."

"Don't make me hurt you."

"You can't hurt me."

Energy forms in my core, ready to be released into the man I love. "Thorne, please. Don't make me do this."

"Give me the grimoire, Elsie." His voice is flat and void of emotion.

"No."

"Then I'll take it." He reaches toward the book, easily unlatching my hands from the cover. I have no strength to fight him. He takes the book and looks me in the eyes. "Goodbye, Elsie. Don't try to find me." Thorne steps away.

"Good boy," a voice says. I turn, finding the familiar

form of Serafina. "Father would be so proud." I watch in horror as Thorne moves to her side with Aaron's grimoire in his grip. He hands the book to his half-sister before turning back toward me.

"This is for the best, Elsie. Trust me." The two of them disappear into the night, leaving me standing alone on the banks of the Ashley River.

I blink several times, hoping reality will return and that what just happened was a figment of my overactive imagination.

"Elsie," Cam's deep voice says through my mind. I turn, finding two wolves standing on the street in plain sight of humans.

"She has him," I whisper. "Serafina has Thorne."

"Where's the grimoire?" Nyssa asks.

"She has that too..." My eyes close, and the world goes black.

the lycan, the witch, and the ward...wait— wrong book

MY EYES OPEN, staring at the ceiling high above my head. Ornate beams, dark with age, run vertically across the room. A decorative brass chandelier hangs in the middle, each bulb cradled in handblown glass. Where the hell am I? Did I pass out? Have I been asleep? That's absurd. I haven't slept in over three hundred years, and vampires don't pass out.

I'm on my feet with my hand on the thick wooden door a heartbeat later. Slowing my movements, I turn the knob, opening it to a nonthreatening hallway. Soft voices ring through the house, and lycan energy fills the rooms. Giving myself a few minutes to acclimate, I recognize the energy instantly. Nyssa and Cam are here.

I move down the stairs with the stealth of a cat. Cam is the first to see me. He's wearing a T-shirt that's at least two sizes too small with the logo "Juicy" stretched tightly across his chest.

"Elsie," he says, standing and moving toward me. "You're okay."

Am I okay? "I think so. What happened?"

"You passed out," Nyssa answers.

"I passed out." I scoff. "I'm a fucking vampire. I don't pass out."

"You might want to tell whoever is in charge of vampire rules that they were wrong. You definitely passed out." Cam moves to my side, offering me an arm and motioning toward a chair.

"I'm good," I refuse help, walking to the same chair. "Phyllis?" I ask, looking around the room.

"She's upstairs, still asleep. Serafina didn't harm her, just morphed into her." Nyssa stands, moving toward a different room. "I have goat's blood in the refrigerator. Let me get some."

I look around, realizing we're in the house where we met Nyssa hours earlier. "How did I get here?"

"I carried you." Cam looks at the wide plank floor under his feet. "When Thorne left with...when he left, you collapsed. I shifted and brought you here."

"You carried me naked?"

Cam smiles, lifting one side of his face higher than the other. "Yeah, sorry. I didn't have a choice."

I try not to think about Cam's private areas touching me. Instead, I focus on the fact that I passed out—something a vampire shouldn't be able to do. "Why did you bring me here?"

"Serafina compromised the wards at your home. We

thought this was our best option for the moment," Nyssa answers, handing me a warm bottle of blood.

Goat's blood usually makes me nauseous, and it takes a while for me to drink an entire bottle. This time, I drain the bottle in one gulp. The richness of flavors covers my palette the entire way down. "Thank you."

"Elsie?" Cam moves back in front of me. "What happened?"

Memories flood my mind, filling me with anxiety. "Thorne took the grimoire."

"He just took it from you?"

"No." I close my eyes at the memory. "He started chanting something I didn't recognize. The shadows surrounding us seemed to dance with his words." I can't fight the tears from falling. "I didn't fight him. I just let him have it."

"You didn't have a choice." Nyssa tries to reassure me.

"There's always a choice," I argue.

"Not when magic is involved." She stands, moving to a bookshelf. "It sounds like Thorne used a compulsion spell on you. You couldn't have fought him if you'd tried."

"I never would've hurt him."

"He knew that." Nyssa opens the book, setting it in front of me. "Are these the words he was chanting?" The spell in front of me is in a language I don't recognize.

"How am I supposed to know?"

Nyssa pulls the book away. "I'm sorry. I thought maybe you could read Latin."

"I was born on a farm in Scotland, where I worked until the day my mother bought passage for a ship bound for Charles Town, South Carolina. For the next one hundred years, I lived in the bowels of a pirate ship where I was tortured, abused, and starved." I stand, moving across the room. "Anything I know, I learned on my own. I'm sorry to disappoint you, but Latin wasn't one of my top priorities."

"So, that means, no?" Cam asks. His words bring me back to the present and the reality of my behavior.

"Nyssa, I'm sorry. That was out of line."

She waves her hands dismissively. "No worries. I understand."

"It doesn't give me permission to be a bitch."

"What the hell kind of nap did I take?" a weak voice says from the staircase landing. "I could've sworn Thorne helped me find a bed in Elsie's house. Now I'm here. Who wants to explain?" Phyllis crosses her arms across her chest.

Cam moves to her side, sliding a long arm around her frail body. "Let me help you."

At his touch, Phyllis's weight magically gives out, and she falls into his arms. "Oh, thank you, Cameron, but it might be better for you to carry me." She wrinkles her forehead at his clothing. "What the hell are you wearing?"

The lycanthrope swoops her into his arms, pulling

her close to his chest as he carries her to the couch we all shared earlier. She makes eye contact with me, wiggling her eyebrows as he pulls away from her clutches. "My clothing choices were limited," he finally answers. "Nyssa is a bit smaller than I am."

"Thank you for helping me, I mean. Not for wearing clothes." She looks between Nyssa and me. "I feel like I've missed the ending of an amazing book." She glances around the room. "Where's Thorne?"

"Phyllis, what was the name of the intern who gave me information on the grimoire?" I refuse to fall victim to Serafina's charades once again.

The elder witch looks at me like I've lost my mind. "Abigail? Does she have something to do with Thorne not being here?"

"No." I sigh before explaining everything that happened, trying to remember every detail and word spoken. "He told you to trust him?" Phyllis asks a few minutes later.

"Aye."

"Why would he do that?"

I shrug. "Because he wanted me to trust him. I don't know what you want me to say." I slam my hands flat on my thighs in frustration.

"What are you thinking, Phyllis?' Nyssa asks.

"I don't know. I haven't known the two of you long, but it seems out of character for him. I've seen the way you communicate. You two are bound to each other through more than trust. You operate as one, often."

She stands, stretching her legs. "Could he have gone with Serafina as a form of protection?"

"Protection of who?" I scoff.

"You," she answers. "I felt that was obvious."

"I can assure you, I don't need protection. I'm stronger than Thorne."

"As a vampire, yes. As a witch, no. With both of those combined, there's no one stronger." Phyllis's words hit hard. She's right. He's stronger than me now.

"Who would he be protecting me from?"

"Serafina," the three of them answer in unison.

"He went with her willingly." My voice is no louder than a whisper. "He gave her Aaron's grimoire."

"Then we'll just have to get it back," Phyllis answers.

"Elsie, I think you were right. Serafina isn't after the binding spell. She could've easily redone that spell in the centuries since." Nyssa reminds me of my words from earlier.

"What are you talking about?" Phyllis asks.

"Elsie thinks Serafina wants a different spell from the grimoire, not the binding spell." Cam fills in the blanks.

"Phyllis, do you know of any other spells Aaron would've held that Serafina would want?" I ask.

The elder witch's face turns pale. "Nothing set in stone, just stories of his magic."

"What aren't you saying?" Nyssa asks, moving closer.

Phyllis sits back on the couch. "My ancestors used to talk about a spell that Aaron was working on to…to siphon death."

"Siphon death?" Cam asks. "What does that mean?"

"Just like it sounds. Aaron tried for years to complete a spell that would siphon death, meaning…he could restore life to the dead."

"Necromancy?" Nyssa asks. "That's forbidden."

"Yes, it's forbidden when life is returned to those who are already dead, not to those who still walk the earth." Phyllis turns toward me with her words. "Aaron was creating a spell to siphon death away from the undead, returning them to life."

Her words hit me in the chest. "He was trying to return life to…to vampires?"

"Yes," she whispers. "He never stopped searching for you."

"A spell that would turn me human? Is that possible?" I look at Phyllis. "Are you sure it's true?"

"No," she reassures me. "It was a story passed down through generations. It could be nothing more than just that, a story."

"Is that something you'd want?" Cam asks. "To be human again?"

"I…I don't know. Why would Serafina want the spell?"

"That's a question I don't have an answer for." Phyllis picks at a loose string on her pants.

I stand, walking toward the oversized fireplace.

"Let's just hypothetically say this is true. Why would Thorne go with her?"

"Because a spell that can transmute death and return a vampire to human has the power to do the opposite," Nyssa answers.

"Meaning Serafina would be able to turn herself into a vampire," Cam adds.

"He's going to stop her." I look each of them in the eye.

Cam looks between the two witches. "What if she binds him before he can stop her? What if he's already bound?"

"Thorne wouldn't be the only one she's able to bind." Phyllis crosses her arms across her chest. "All of us would be bound too."

"We can't do this alone," I announce.

"Look around, Elsie. We're the strongest of our kind. There is no one else." Phyllis's words sound angry.

"There are many who are stronger than me. Four in particular." I close my eyes, knowing the information I'm about to divulge could end with the death of an immortal child.

"Who?" Cam asks. "Amelia and Topher are the strongest in existence."

"The children," I answer. "There are four of them. Each holds magic in their blood and the strength of a vampire."

"Children are no match for Serafina." Nyssa scoffs.

"These are."

"Are these the same children who are being held captive by the Goddess of the Sea?" Phyllis asks.

"Aye, one and the same."

"Holy fuck," Cam says, running a hand through his hair. "You want us to save four immortal children vampires from the Goddess of the Sea?"

"Technically, three. I know where the fourth one is. He's safe…or was the last I knew."

"How do you suggest we fight the goddess?" The look on Nyssa's face is almost comedic.

"Can you make my power stronger?"

The witches share a look. "Yes, but Elsie, the power in your blood isn't the same. Yes, you have magic, but not to the same extreme as Thorne. It will never be as strong as his."

"I don't care. Anything will help."

"There is a spell," Nyssa says, moving out of the room. She returns minutes later, carrying a book similar in age to Aaron's. "This is my family grimoire." She flips through the pages, landing on the one she wants. She sighs. "My ancestor created a spell to pull energy and strength from the world around us."

"Do it," I demand.

"There's only one problem. The power, if it doesn't kill you, can only be used one time. After that, it's gone."

"Do it," I repeat.

Cam raises his hand. "What are we up against? How powerful is this goddess?"

"She's a goddess," I answer truthfully. "However, she owes me a favor."

"A favor for what?" Phyllis asks.

"I killed her husband. That has to count for something."

"Am I the only one who's confused?" Cam asks, making me smile.

"No," the witches answer in unison.

I look around the room, making eye contact with each person. "You're going to have to trust me."

"Hell, I don't have anything to lose anyway. I'm in." Phyllis moves to my side.

"Shit, me, too," Cam says with a sigh, moving to my other side.

"Nyssa, I understand if you don't join. You have a job here that needs you."

The lycanthrope closes her eyes. "This job is kind of boring anyway. I'll make arrangements to have the library shifted to its hiding spot." She moves closer. "What's the next step?"

"We're going to New Orleans."

things aren't always what they seem

ARRANGING the private jet is much easier than I expected. One call to Amelia and the plane is set to pick us up in thirty minutes.

"Remind me again what's in New Orleans," Phyllis says, standing in the middle of the living area of Nyssa's home. She shakes her head. "I know it's the fourth immortal child, but what's so special about this kid."

"His name is Brayden, and he holds more power than anyone I've come in contact with in my three hundred years."

"He's going to help us get the others?" Cam asks, carrying a bundle of books.

"Aye. Before you ask, there is no plan."

Nyssa claps her hands loudly. "This is going to be fun."

"Are we ready?" I ask our small crew. We file

through the door in single file and load into Phyllis's SUV.

"How'd my car get here?" she asks, climbing behind the wheel.

"The same way you did," I answer.

"Got it—unconscious." Phyllis backs out of the driveway, turning us toward the local airport.

"The plane will be waiting on the tarmac," I announce as we pull into the parking lot. We unload, carrying a few small bags, and enter the local airport. Just as Amelia promised, the jet is sitting at the end of the runway with its door standing open and stairs leading to the concrete below. "That's us," I point at the private jet.

"I don't have friends with jets. Who are these people?" Phyllis asks.

"That belongs to my sister-in-law," Cam interrupts. "Her maker gave it to her." He scoffs as the witches stare at him expectantly. "It's a long story, but she's got more money than she knows what to do with."

"I like her already," Phyllis answers.

"Welcome aboard." A tall woman with bright blue hair greets us. She's wearing a pair of sweatpants and a sweatshirt that matches the hue of her hair. "Hey, y'all. Find a seat, and buckle up. We'll be on our way shortly."

The four of us follow directions, sitting in the extravagant cabin. I sink into the leather of the seat, remembering Thorne was with me the last time I was on this plane. I fight the sadness that fills me at the thought of not being with him.

"Hey, again. I'm Terri, and I'll be your flight attendant today." The blue-haired woman waves as she speaks.

"You're a lycanthrope?" I ask, sensing her energy.

"I am. And you're a vampire." She looks around the plane, pointing at Cam and Phyllis. "Lycanthrope and witch." She turns her attention toward Nyssa. "What the hell are you? I feel lycan energy, but there's something else."

"I'm a witch and lycan hybrid," Nyssa answers.

"Well, damn. Didn't know there was such a thing."

"How have we never met?" Cam asks our chatty attendant.

"Oh, I'm new to the area. I'm from Mississippi and decided to move to the Big Easy for a change of scenery." Terri sniffs the air in front of her. "You smell like Christopher."

"He's my brother," Cam answers.

"Ah. I've got a lot to learn." She motions to the seatbelt sign. "Buckle up and hold on. If y'all don't mind, I'm not going to go through all the safety protocols. You know what to do."

Two minutes later, we're off the ground and heading toward New Orleans. "I think it might be time for a plan," Phyllis announces once we're in the air.

"What plan are y'all talking about?" our flight attendant asks. She slides close to Nyssa and clasps her hands together. "I love a good plan." Her behavior feels off.

"*I don't trust her,*" I announce through my mind. In unison, Nyssa and Phyllis nod, telling me they agree.

"We don't need a plan." I scoff. "We'll just wing it." Cam looks at each of us with a confused look. I casually nod toward Terri, making sure he sees my action. His eyebrows raise in understanding.

"I agree. Winging it is always the best." Cam stretches his long legs in front of him, crossing them at the ankle. "I'm going to take a nap. Wake me when we land."

"What's bringing y'all to New Orleans?" Terri asks.

"Cam's giving us a tour of the sights," Nyssa lies.

"Well, you know us old people. We need a plan." Phyllis scoffs, extending Nyssa's lie. "I'm old and don't do well wandering around in a new city."

"Oh, honey. New Orleans is easy to get around in. It's just a huge grid." Terri slides into the seat next to Phyllis. "I can show y'all around if you'd like."

"Actually, I'd like something to drink." Phyllis smiles an empty smile. "There are drinks on this plane, aren't there?"

"Of course. Let me get you something." Terri stands, moving toward the back of the jet.

"A bottle of water, please. And make sure it's sealed. I'm weird about drinking from previously opened containers," Phyllis calls after our flight attendant.

"We'll be on the ground in thirty minutes. We'll talk when we're alone," I reassure everyone.

"Here you go, honey. Let me know if you need anything else." Terri hands a full bottle of water to Phyllis. "If you need a tour guide while you're in town, I'd be happy to oblige. I don't have many friends since moving there."

"So you've said. We'll keep that in mind," Nyssa answers.

My phone rings, drawing my attention away from the strange lycanthrope. The name across the screen surprises me.

"Hello?"

"Elsie? Is everything okay?"

I smile. *"Of course. We're almost to New Orleans. Thank you for the plane, by the way."*

"You can't land," Amelia answers. *"Something is going on. It's not safe."*

"What are you talking about?" I focus on keeping the smile on my face, hoping not to alert the rest of the plane.

"Don't say anything else," she warns. *"Just listen."*

"That sounds great," I continue the facade.

"Most of the vampire community in the city has gone under some sort of a...trance. That's not the best description, but it's the only way to describe it at the moment."

"Wow, that will be fun."

Amelia laughs at my wording. *"From what I can tell,*

vampires who don't drink human blood are immune to whatever is going on."

"Yeah, our lycanthrope flight attendant is doing a great job." I close my eyes, hoping Amelia picks up on my meaning.

"It's affecting some lycan, too. Only the ones that have eaten raw meat in the past few weeks. Topher is fine. Look behind your lycanthrope's right ear. Everyone affected has a small, moon-shaped mole that's suddenly appeared."

"That's too bad," I continue. *"Hopefully, they'll feel better soon."*

"I know you're coming after Brayden. I've arranged for Fran to meet you at the airport with the boy. Pick them up and go anywhere but here. Get them to safety."

I laugh awkwardly. *"That's hilarious. I'll be sure to tell Cam that."*

"Shit. Cam's with you?"

"He is. He wanted to crash our girls' trip."

"Is he okay?"

"Yes, that's great," I answer.

"When you land, get rid of the flight attendant. I don't care what you have to do. The pilot is human. He won't be affected."

"Understood."

"Elsie, be safe."

"I will," I respond before hanging up the phone.

"That sounded intense," Terri says from the far end of the plane.

"Just a friend waiting for us to land," I lie. I move to

the lycanthrope at vampire speed, pulling back her blue hair. Just as Amelia described, a moon-shaped mole sits underneath her ear. Shit.

"What are you doing?" Terri asks, turning suddenly.

"Have you always had this mole?"

"What are you talking about?" She rubs her fingers across the dark spot. "I don't have a mole."

"Ladies and gentlemen," the pilot interrupts, "we will be landing in New Orleans in ten minutes. Please return to your seats and prepare for landing."

I look the lycanthrope in the eyes. "When we land, you're going to leave this plane."

"When we land, I'm going to leave the plane," she repeats.

"You're going to walk away and forget that you saw us," I continue.

"I'm going to walk away and forget I saw you."

"When asked about your trip, you're going to tell them we found alternate transportation." She repeats my words.

"Why am I doing this?" she whispers.

"Because the alternative is your death." I don't mince my words.

"I understand," she answers. Slowly, her pupils return to their normal size.

Without question, I feel the energy of Phyllis, Cam, and Nyssa behind me. As the plane descends on the runway, Phyllis and Nyssa sit while Cam and I stand watch over Terri. "Can you get her off the plane? I'm going to talk to the pilot."

"After you, ma'am," Cam says, helping Terri to her feet while I head into the cockpit.

"Two passengers are about to join us, and we need to take off immediately. Is that possible?"

The pilot stares at me in confusion. "Ms. Lockhart said we would be staying in New Orleans."

"There's been a change of plan. Ms. Lockhart reassured me that you would understand."

The older man nods his head slightly. "Of course. Where are we going?"

"I'm afraid I can't let you know that until we're in the air."

"Okay," he answers. "This is going to be fun."

I return to the cabin to find Cam and Terri gone. Through the lowered stairs, I catch a glimpse of the boy I haven't seen since he was human and his vampire nanny. He lifts his nose into the air, sniffing the air around him. *"Hello, Elsie,"* he says through my mind.

"Hello, Brayden. Is it really you?"

A soft laugh resonates through my mind. *"Of course, it's me, silly."*

"Lower your shield," I demand. *"I need to feel that it's you."*

On command, energy floods toward me. It's the familiar energy I recognize from the young boy who tragically lost both parents simply because he was gifted. *"It's you. Thank you, Brayden."*

Fran and Brayden are standing at the door of the jet, a heartbeat later. "You're welcome, Elsie." The immortal child moves in front of me, wrapping his small arms around my waist. "It's good to see you."

"Aye, you, too." I smile, returning his hug.

"Elsie," Fran, Brayden's elderly vampire nanny, greets me. "You look like shit."

"Thanks." I laugh. "It's been a rough few days."

"Amelia demanded we meet you here and be ready to leave the city. I don't know what's going on, but I know it's for Brayden's protection."

"Who are you?" Brayden asks, standing in front of Nyssa and Phyllis.

"I'm Phyllis." The elder witch greets the immortal child.

"I'm Nyssa..."

"*What* are you?" Brayden interrupts.

"I'm a hybrid. Half witch and half lycan."

"May I?" Brayden brings Nyssa's hand to his nose. "You're more than that."

"I don't know what you mean." She pulls her hand away.

I stare at the woman whom I quickly trusted. "Nyssa, what's he talking about?"

"I...I don't know."

Brayden stares at the beautiful lycanthrope. "Yes, she does." I step between the boy and the hybrid. "I can feel the energy in you."

"Brayden, do I need to..."

"No," he answers quickly. "She's not going to harm anyone. At least not any of us."

"What is he talking about?" Nyssa asks, stepping around me.

"What are you keeping from us?" Phyllis joins the interrogation.

Cam climbs back on the plane. "We have visitors." He jokes. "Hello, visitors. I'm Cameron St. James."

"Hello, I'm Brayden." The immortal child shakes Cam's hand dramatically.

"And I'm Fran. It seems we're joining you for your trip." Fran turns to Brayden, pointing him toward an empty seat. "Why don't we sit down?"

"Not until he tells me what he's talking about." I stop his movement. "Brayden, what do I need to know about Nyssa?" I'm done playing nice. Serafina has tricked me twice, and now she has Thorne. I'll be damned if I'll let her make it three times.

Brayden and Nyssa make eye contact and seem to have some sort of silent conversation. One that even my abilities don't allow me to hear.

"The boy is right. I'm more than just a witch." Energy balls in my core, ready to fight whatever is about to happen. Nyssa sighs deeply. "I'm not going to hurt anyone. I would've done that long before now."

"Your time is running out, Nyssa," I warn.

"She's a druid," Brayden says from his seat.

"A druid?" I repeat. "What the hell is a druid?"

"I'm only half druid. My father was a lycanthrope,

meaning I'm still a hybrid. However, my mother wasn't just a witch, and our power wasn't handed down through generations. We are the last of our kind." Nyssa's voice sounds defeated as she admits her heritage.

"What does that mean?" Cam asks.

"It means my power comes from the elements around me. Unlike you and Phyllis, I can control all the elements—water, earth, air, and fire. Because I am half lycan, I am particularly good at lunar magic. Through my druid heritage, my power comes from the earth. Through my lycan heritage, I am tethered to the moon, allowing me to draw from and control its power."

"Why hide what you are?" I ask.

"Through history, I've been forced to hide who and what I truly am. To the world, I'm a lycanthrope and practicing witch, blending into the shadows that surround me. Druids are relics, ghosts of a lost age, hunted until there's nothing left but whispers of their existence. It should stay that way. Druids were dangerous wielders of an old untamed magic that could call forests to rise and rivers to rage. If anyone found out, if they even suspected, I'd be hunted down, just like the others, just like the old days. The druid blood in my veins is a target. I've buried those abilities, masked them in the strength of the wolf and witch, never daring to call on the full extent of the magic within me. It's the only way to stay alive in a world that would see me as a threat—a living relic they'd want to bury for good."

The cabin is quiet as Nyssa's words sink in. "Damn," Cam interrupts the silence. "That was deep."

"How did you know, Brayden?" I ask the immortal child.

He shrugs. "She felt different."

"Nyssa? In the grand scheme of things, what does this mean?"

"Elsie, weren't you listening?" Brayden's young voice asks. "She can control the moon, which controls the tides, which can control the Goddess of the Sea."

"Which means we can get the children," I add.

"Yes," Brayden answers. "I'm ready to go if you are."

On cue, the jet begins to taxi, taking us to a yet-to-be-determined destination. I sit on the other side of Brayden, unsure what to think. There are still so many unanswered questions, but for now, luck seems to be on our side.

a world beyond

ONCE THE JET is safely in the air, Phyllis asks the question I imagine everyone wants to know. "What the hell was wrong with Terri?"

"I don't know," I answer truthfully. "Amelia didn't want us to stay in New Orleans and insisted we get Fran and Brayden out quickly."

"Did she say what's going on?" Cam asks, sliding forward in his seat.

I look at the lycanthrope whose entire family is in the city. "She said that some of the vampires had come under some sort of trance."

"A trance? What does that mean?" Phyllis asks.

"It's not just the vampires. Some of the lycan have too." I turn toward Cam. "Topher's fine. Amelia didn't mention anything about the rest of your brothers."

Nyssa and Cam share a look. "Why only some of them?" she asks.

"Amelia said the vampires who don't drink human blood were not affected and that only the lycan who had eaten raw meat in the past few weeks were under the 'trance.'" I use finger quotes.

"You think Terri was affected?" Phyllis asks.

"Amelia told me to look for a moon-shaped mole behind her right ear. Terri had the mark."

"Holy shit," Fran says for the first time. "Oh, I'm sorry, Brayden. Excuse my language."

"I've heard bad words before," Brayden reassures his nanny. He looks at the rest of us. "It's not a trance."

"Brayden? Do you know something about what's going on?"

He looks at the two witches. "It's a spell, and it's not just in New Orleans."

The realization of his words hits me in the gut. "Serafina," I whisper. "Is it possible?"

"I think it's more than possible," Nyssa answers.

"Can someone fill me in on what's going on?" Fran asks, sliding forward. "Who is Serafina, and what does she have to do with the trance?"

The four of us spend the next few minutes recalling every detail of what's happened in Charleston, starting with our first encounter with Serafina and her illusion magic and ending with her and Thorne leaving together.

"Thorne left with this woman, willingly?" Fran asks.

I fight the tears welling in my eyes. "Aye."

"Oh, honey. I'm so sorry." She moves to my side, wrapping her arms around me.

For the first time since watching him walk away, I allow the emotions that have filled me to flow. Tears slide down my cheeks as I bury my head into Fran's petite shoulder. The old Elsie would never have allowed herself to feel this much emotion. The old Elsie would've never allowed anyone to see her weakness.

Fran pulls away only after the tears stop. "Elsie. I feel like I know both you and Thorne pretty well. We fought together, nearly died together, and survived together." She puts her hands on my shoulders. "Thorne spent two hundred years searching for you. Hell, he had himself turned into a vampire so he could find you." Deep brown eyes look into mine. "He would never willingly leave you."

"He was under the spell." Brayden fills in the blank.

"There's only one flaw with that theory." I interrupt. "He doesn't drink human blood. The spell wouldn't have bound him."

"Except he did." Nyssa stands, moving to our side. "He drank my blood at the ritual."

I step away from Fran. Oh, my God. She's right. He drank human blood right before he started acting strange. "He's under her control." The weight of a thousand elephants lifts off my shoulders. "We have to get to him. We have to save him."

"We will," Cam answers. "But we're going to need all the help we can get before we go in there, guns blazing. If Thorne's under her control, he's not going to be on our side." He nods to Brayden's seat. "If all the kids are like him, we need them. Their abilities, combined with Nyssa's magic, are the only chance we have."

"The hot lycanthrope is right. We can't do this alone." Phyllis joins the conversation. "We need the kids. I say we stick to the original plan."

"We never had a plan." I remind everyone.

"It's about damn time to get one." Phyllis moves to Brayden's side. "You are an amazing young man."

"Thank you." He smiles widely, revealing a large gap in his front teeth where, before becoming a vampire, his baby teeth had fallen out. Seeing his toothless grin reminds me of his stolen childhood, along with the three waiting to be rescued.

"Where are the children?" Nyssa asks no one in particular.

"They're on Eudora's island," Brayden answers as if it's common knowledge.

Everyone on the plane turns toward the immortal child. "Her island?" I ask. "Where is Eudora's island?"

He shrugs. "It changes every day."

"That makes no sense," Fran answers.

"Sure, it does. Eudora is the Goddess of the Sea. She can make it go anywhere she wants. Most of the time, it's hidden in other dimensions."

"Other dimensions?" I repeat Brayden's words, not sure I heard him correctly.

"She mostly keeps the island hidden between the dimensions or realms," he continues.

Cam sighs. "How are we supposed to find something that hides in a place we don't know how to get to?"

Brayden slides forward on the leather seat, his feet lowering to the floor in front of him. "It appears every day during high tide."

"Brayden, how do you know all of this?" Fran asks.

He sighs. "I don't know. I just think about it, and the answers are there."

"When it appears during high tide, does it appear in the same location every day?" Phyllis asks.

The immortal child sits silent for a few minutes. "I think so. It's like a short time when she can't hide." He turns toward the elderly witch. "I know I'm only a child, but I'm not lying to you. What would be the purpose of that? I have nothing to gain from lying. Thorne is my friend. So is Alex. I want to help them."

"How?" Phyllis whispers.

"He can read our thoughts. Sorry, I probably should've mentioned that before now," I answer.

Brayden turns toward Nyssa. "It would explain a lot, wouldn't it?"

"What's he talking about?" Cam asks Nyssa.

She shakes her head. "Nothing. I was just wondering what the boy's heritage is."

Brayden pulls a piece of paper from the bag he's carrying. "The island will appear at these coordinates during high tide." He scribbles down a line of numbers before handing the paper to me.

I stare at the sequence of numbers in front of me. There is no doubt that Brayden is a genius and holds more power than anyone I know, but trusting something like this to him seems—dangerous. What if he's wrong? Am I willing to stake Thorne's life on what an eight-year-old says to be true? There's more than Thorne's life in the balance.

"Trust me, Elsie," Brayden says with a smile. "I don't know how I know it's true, but I do."

I close my eyes, willing the answers to come. "I don't want to make this decision alone." I turn toward my new friends. "What do you all think?"

The three of them stand awkwardly quiet. "I don't think anyone feels comfortable making this decision," Cam answers several seconds later.

"We're out of time," I remind them. "This is the only lead we have to go on. Since Eudora took the children, I've been unable to find any information on where she possibly took them."

"A glimmer of hope is better than nothing," Phyllis says. "If this is our only option, then we take it. I've only known the boy for half an hour, but I trust him." She turns, facing the toothless immortal child. "Goddess, forgive me, I trust him."

"Agreed," Cam says.

"Nyssa?"

"Me, too." Her voice is barely audible. "I trust him."

I turn, heading into the cockpit with the coordinates in hand. "Ms. Abernathy," the pilot greets me. "Do we have a location?"

I hand him the paper. "How far away is this?"

He feeds the numbers into a computer, pulling up what looks like a flight path. "Not too far." He points to an area in the middle of the water. "This is where the coordinates are taking us. Are you sure this is where you want to go?"

"Yes. Can you get us there?"

He sighs. "I will have enough fuel to get you there, but obviously, there will be no place to land." He turns toward me, looking me in the eyes. "Are you expecting something to be there?"

"Aye. An island."

"If you want to go onto the island, you're going to have to jump."

"Okay," I whisper. "We can do that."

I watch as he pushes a few buttons on the computer before turning the plane hard to the right. "Looks like a three-hour flight."

"Thank you." I turn, leaving him alone, returning to the cabin to find five pairs of curious eyes. "We'll be there in three hours."

"What if we don't arrive during high tide?" Fran asks.

"Then we make it high tide," Brayden answers. "Right, Nyssa?"

She closes her eyes. "Right," she whispers.

"Nyssa, I need to know that you're all in. We can't do this without you. If you're not 100 percent with us, we need to know now."

She shakes her head. "I'm in. Brayden is right. I can control the lunar phase, which will make the tide rise, and theoretically, the island will become visible."

"Three hours is close to high tide." Cam pulls his phone away from his face. "The natural high tide will be close to being in effect by the time we arrive. That, combined with Nyssa's ability, should make the island visible."

"Get some rest," I suggest to my new friends. "I have a feeling we're going to need as much strength as possible."

"This is sounding more adventurous by the minute." Phyllis's words make me laugh. She's right. This is going to be rough, and it's only the first battle of our war. I sit on the other side of Brayden, relishing his warm energy. I don't know if he's covering me with warmth somehow or if it's his natural energy I'm feeling. Whatever the case, I'm enjoying it.

"You should drink two bottles of blood," Brayden says, handing me a bottle from his backpack.

"What about you?"

"I'm full." He pats his stomach dramatically.

I glance at Fran, hoping for reassurance. "He ate before we got on the plane."

I down the bottle in one gulp. Brayden was right. I was hungry. We sit in silence while the lycan and witch rest. In the quiet of the moment, I can't help but think how different my life is from where it started.

As a child, I never went further than a mile from the spot where I was born. As a vampire, I've been all over the world many times, lived a life of horror and luxury, and seen so much history that I could write several books. Now, I'm on the way to an island that moves between dimensions, where a goddess is holding three immortal children captive and being led to the island by an immortal child with immeasurable power. In our lives, we have moments that define who and what we truly are. This is mine.

Brayden is busy drawing in a sketchbook he pulled out of his bag. "What are you working on?" I ask the immortal child.

"A map."

I take longer to study the details. "Is that a map of the island?"

"Yeah. I can see it in my mind. Kind of like looking down from the air."

"You're using the power of air," Nyssa says, moving to the seat across from him. "You have the ability to draw upon all the powers of earth, Brayden—like me."

It takes a minute for her words to sink in. "You think he's a druid?"

"I do." Nyssa nods at the child. "So does he."

"Is that true, Brayden?"

He shrugs. "It makes sense."

"Did your parents have your abilities?"

Brayden stares at the paper in front of him. "I don't think so. I never noticed if they did." He looks up, making eye contact with Nyssa. "They died."

"I'm sorry," she answers.

"I know." Brayden turns toward me. "Elsie, I'm okay with being a vampire. My life wasn't stolen from me. I've seen what's going to happen in my future." He smiles, not offering any more information.

"You're pretty awesome," I whisper, ruffling his perfectly styled blonde hair.

"I know." He hands me a map that looks like it came from a master cartographer. "The island isn't very big. These are the furthest points, and this is where the castle is."

"Of course, it's a castle."

"What are these?" I point at his drawing of long reed-looking items. "It looks like seaweed."

"I think that's what it is. It hides the island from view. They kind of alter perception."

"Brayden, is this possible?"

He sits in silence for a few minutes before nodding. "Yes."

"Ladies and gentlemen. We will be above the coordinates in five minutes. I can get the plane low enough to depressurize, but will only be able to maintain that speed for thirty seconds." Anxiety fills the pilot's voice. "Time will not be on our side."

"Can you hide us?" I ask the immortal child. He nods in response. "I've been doing it the entire trip. It's easy now."

I stand, facing the rest of our makeshift crew. "Cam, Nyssa, you're with me. Phyllis, you will stay on the plane with Fran and Brayden."

"Like hell, I will," Phyllis argues. "I didn't come all this way to be coddled like an old fart. I'm a witch, for goddess's sake. Let me do something amazing before I die. If I die here, then I will have died bravely."

"You won't be able to fight her."

"I deserve a chance to try," she retorts.

"Two minutes." The captain's voice rings over the speaker.

"Elsie?" Brayden calls across the jet. "I feel Alex. They're here."

"I'm coming," Phyllis whispers. "I'm responsible for myself. I won't be a burden."

"Okay." I instantly regret my words. A beep emanating from the cockpit echoes through the cabin of the jet. One glance out the window tells me we are flying dangerously low.

"Nyssa?"

The hybrid closes her eyes, and the sky turns black. Her arms raise to her sides and begin moving smoothly in the air. Watching her reminds me of a conductor in charge of a full symphony, molding and shaping the notes to their will.

Cam pushes the door open, filling the cabin with wind. As Nyssa continues conducting, the water below follows. "There's nothing out there," Phyllis says.

"It's there," Brayden says from my side. "Look." He points through the murky sea. For a brief moment, I catch a glimpse of something that looks like land. "You have to trust," he whispers.

I close my eyes and leap.

the battle of a lifetime

MY FEET HIT solid ground seconds later. Vampires can't drown, but swimming to the nearest landmass isn't high on my list of things to do. Not far behind me lands a large black wolf with piercing green eyes. I don't know when Nyssa shifted, but it was a smart decision. A few yards away, an even larger wolf lands with Phyllis clinging to its back. Brayden's undeniable energetic shield is still surrounding us, hopefully keeping us hidden as long as possible.

Nyssa and I join Cam and Phyllis, and the four of us hide behind an oversized boulder. Phyllis rolls her neck slightly. "That was a little rougher than I expected."

"Are you alright?" I ask.

"Yeah, just a little stiff. I've never ridden a wolf before." She wiggles her eyebrows, lightening the situation. "Next time, I'll have to try it in human form."

I glance up, seeing the tail of the plane as it lifts into

the clouds. I don't know how long the shield will hold, but we need to be prepared for anything. Pulling the hand-drawn map out of my pocket, I point to the spot where Brayden felt Alex's energy. "This is our target."

"Are we just going to knock on the door?" Phyllis asks.

"Why don't I feel anything?" Cam asks through my mind. *"There's no energy here. I don't even feel you."*

"Brayden," I answer aloud. "He's covered us with an invisible shield."

"That's not going to last much longer."

"I told you we needed a plan." Phyllis scoffs.

"We haven't had a plan yet. Why start now?" I smile, hoping to reassure the elderly witch.

"That's not helping." Nyssa shifts back into human form. Standing in front of everyone fully naked. Phyllis scoffs, slapping her thighs with the palms of her hands. "Well, there you go. Now we are even more threatening."

"I don't need clothes to threaten anyone. My powers are stronger when there are no barriers between me and the elements." Nyssa turns toward the small castle. "She's inside."

"How?" I ask.

"I can pull down Brayden's shield." Without another word, Nyssa begins moving. The three of us follow, not sure what's about to happen.

We stand at what looks like a door. A naked woman, a large wolf, a pissed-off vampire, and an elderly witch—the perfect characters for a children's book. Imagining the cover with artwork of our current state brings a smile to my face.

Nyssa knocks her fists heavily on the wooden facade. In a heartbeat, the door disappears, as does the castle. Standing in the middle of barren rock is the goddess we're here to see, Eudora.

"Look what the cat dragged in," she says with a laugh. "I mean that honestly because it looks like you brought everything except a cat, or are they running a bit late?" She's wearing what looks like a cape, covering skin-tight spandex. Long blonde hair hangs down her back, with loose curls hanging over her shoulders. Even though she doesn't look any older than me, no doubt she's been around a few millennia. "I must say, I'm impressed." She crosses her arms in front of her chest. "I don't know how you found me, but here we are."

"Cat woman called; she wants her clothes back." Phyllis's words make me smile.

"We're here for the children," I answer. In an instant, Brayden's shield disappears, filling me with the energy of the multi-dimensional island, Eudora, and something that brings tears to my eyes—Alex.

"The children aren't here," she answers.

"You're lying," Phyllis argues.

Eudora wrinkles her forehead. "You brought your grandma?" Anger rolls from Phyllis. Thankfully, she doesn't do anything stupid. The Goddess of the Sea looks around our small group. "I know what he is." She points at Cam. "And everyone knows what you are. The smell of Kragen's blood in your veins is nauseating." She turns her attention toward Nyssa. "You're something new." She stalks closer. "You smell familiar yet ancient at the same time."

"Stop stalling, Eudora. I feel Alex. Hand him and the girls over, or we will be forced to kill you."

Eudora's laugh echoes off the rocks. "I don't know what's more entertaining. The fact that you brought a raggedy wolf and your grandma with you, or that you actually believe you stand a chance against me."

"I did what you wanted. Kragen is dead."

"You were just a means to an end." She scoffs. "The children are the true prize."

"Alex?" I call through my mind.

"I'm afraid he can't hear you, dear."

"Alex? I'm here. Where are you?"

Eudora crosses her arms in front of her chest. "You're either stubborn or stupid. I'm not sure which."

"We're not leaving without them," Nyssa hisses.

"So be it." Eudora warns. "I'm bored with this. It seems every conversation that involves Elsbeth is rather on the boring side."

"It must be my quick wit," I retort.

"I just realized you're missing someone." Eudora smiles. "Where's the handsome captain?" She pretends to pout. "Oh, boo-hoo. Don't tell me there's been a rift between the two of you. Or even better, he's joined

Kragen." I stare at the beautiful woman, refusing to answer.

"Give us the children," Phyllis says, stepping to the side.

"Witch, you have no power here." Eudora waves her hand, commanding a thin piece of seaweed from out of nowhere. It wraps around Phyllis's thin body, trapping her hands at her sides and covering her mouth and eyes. "See how easy that was?"

I rip the bindings from Phyllis, freeing her from Eudora's magic. "We need to get her away from the water," the elderly witch whispers. "The water is her strength."

"We won't leave the children," I retort.

"Then we take the water away from her." Nyssa's words echo through my mind. *"Phyllis, I need your help. Can you cast a few spells to keep the water from returning?"*

"I can try," Phyllis answers. Her soft chanting begins moments later.

Nyssa raises her hands high above her head. Her body begins to transform, not into the wolf we're accustomed to seeing, but into something I have no words for. Her body elongates, her skin shifting and taking on a sleek, glossy dark sheen. Her arms stretch to her sides, morphing into graceful, massive fins. Long legs fuse, transforming into a powerful tale that slaps against the rock and shakes it underneath our feet.

Her face softens, and her features become otherworldly, and her once-green eyes become dark, like the depths of the ocean she came from.

"Holy shit," Cam's words echo through my mind.

"Agreed."

Her power is overwhelming as she turns her gaze on the goddess. "That's what I felt in you." Eudora spews. "Druid."

Nyssa opens her mouth, releasing a deep rumble as she leaps from the island into the water below.

"What the hell is she doing?" Phyllis stops chanting long enough to ask.

"I don't know, but she's managed to distract Eudora." I turn toward the lycanthrope. "Cam?"

"On it." He takes advantage of her distraction, leaping onto her back and physically knocking her to the ground. Sharp claws rake across her face, leaving deep marks in their wake. He retreats seconds later as she turns, ready to fight.

"Phyllis, keep going." I encourage, just as I join Cam, moving in front of her with lightning speed. "Burn," I whisper, standing inches behind her back. On cue, a circle of flames engulfs her, pulling the water even further away.

"Bitch!" Eudora yells as a blast of water dissolves the flames. "I'm the Goddess of the Sea. Do you think a little fire is going to hurt me?"

Cam repeats his motion from earlier, this time knocking her legs from underneath her. Eudora falls, hitting the rocks beneath with a thud.

"Burn," I whisper again, this time catching the bottom of her cape on fire.

The goddess stands, sweeping her arms toward the flames. Instead of the water that flowed earlier, nothing happens. She tries once more, receiving the same result. "What have you done?" Her face contorts, changing from the beautiful face of Eudora into a creature from the depths of the abyss.

Like Nyssa, her arms transform into massive fins. The soft curves of her human form are replaced by the sleek, scaled bulk of a leviathan. She raises her head, roaring so deep it resonates through my body and to the water below. She's no longer a goddess, walking among mortals. She has become the sea itself.

"Phyllis?" The elder witch continues chanting, her voice crescendoing, matching the noise around her. Magic flows from her frail body.

Eudora slides into the water just as a large monster breaches the surface—Nyssa. She's transformed from the sleek whale-like creature she was earlier into something from a fable.

"Control the water," Nyssa's words echo through my mind. *"We have to remove her from her element."*

I stand in awe as Nyssa rises from the water. The top of her body transforms into her familiar human form. She raises her head to the moon and howls. On demand, the moon responds, growing three times its size. Her arms begin to conduct, drawing the waves to her command.

Eudora swims into Nyssa's bottom half, knocking her slightly to the side. Instead of fighting, Nyssa remains focused on the moon, calling it, forcing it to bend to her will.

For the first time in a long while, I feel completely helpless. Cam moves to my side, and we watch the spectacle in front of us unfold.

Nyssa's eyes open and return to their bright green hue. *"Lend your strength to Phyllis. Both of you. Draw the water away. Her power comes from the water. Take her away from the water, and she's nothing but a weakened immortal."*

Cam shakes his head, transforming back into human form. Moving quickly to Phyllis, we flank her on either side. I close my eyes, allowing energy to flow through me.

"What are we doing?" Cam asks.

"Use your magic," Nyssa whispers through my mind.

Cam lays a hand on Phyllis's shoulder. I copy his movement from the other side. The moment the three of us make contact, my body jolts in response. Drawing on the power in my core, I focus on imagining the water pulling away from the island, leaving nothing except dry land in its wake.

I have no idea if I'm doing anything correctly. The picture in my mind feels right. *"That's it,"* Nyssa whispers. *"Keep going."*

Opening my eyes, I'm surprised to see what I envisioned taking place in front of me. The water that raged around the island is now calm and receding. Seeing the outcome gives me the strength to continue. In my mind's eye, I imagine the water moving further away, leaving Eudora's transformed figure lying on a bed of wet sand.

"Phyllis, hold the water back. Cam and Elsie, I need you —now!"

I don't hesitate. Cam shifts into wolf form, and the two of us run toward the beached sea creature and Nyssa, back in human form. Leaping from the side of the island, we land on either side of the druid, staring down the leviathan.

Like a well-oiled machine, Cam and I move simultaneously on either side of the Eudora. The wolf is on top of her a heartbeat later, his teeth sinking into thick flesh. I copy his movement, tearing thick scales from her deformed body.

She roars, the sound echoing off the barren land surrounding her. A long tail whips through the air, striking me in the back and throwing me several yards away. Pushing off the sand, I realize the water has completely drained, forming a basin of hot sand below. Instead of the middle of the ocean, we're in a desert. What the hell?

One glance at Nyssa tells me she's the force behind the change. Still in human form, her arms are stretched high above her head, crafting the imagery of a dome. Turning back toward Eudora, I realize she's done just that. The Leviathan is surrounded by a dome of fire, the one element capable of keeping the water at bay.

*"Kill her,"*_Nyssa's words ring through my head. *"She's weakened by the loss of water. Kill her—now!"*

I don't hesitate. Running full speed, I pass through the dome without hesitation. Cam does the same, coming through slightly singed. Copying Nyssa's moves, I lift my hands above my head, drawing on the power that flows through me. "Burn!" I yell at the creature.

As if controlled by my words, fire leaps from the dome to the monster in front of me. The roar of Eudora's pain, mixed with confusion, vibrates every part of my body. I refuse to release her from my grip. Forming my hands into fists, I envision the fire flowing from hand to hand. The creature makes eye contact with me once more as I pull my hands apart, spreading the fire between them.

"Goodbye, Eudora," I whisper before throwing enough fire at the goddess to burn her alive. Her body is engulfed in an instant as she screams once more. Cam jumps on top of her head, ripping and tearing into the remains of her flesh. His body somehow managing to steer clear of direct flames. The leviathan's screams become softer as the creature sways slightly from side to side, eventually collapsing in a wet thud on the desert floor.

"I can't hold it much longer," Phyllis's weak voice says through my mind.

"Get out of there!" Nyssa yells.

I'm just about to follow directions when Eudora swipes her tail one last time, knocking Cam to the sand unconscious. "Cam!" I scream, moving to his side.

"I'm sorry," Phyllis's soft voice says.

Without thought, I pick up the lycanthrope's shifted body, lifting him high above my head. I envision Kragen and his ability to defy gravity by flying. Closing my eyes, I pull on the energy inside and lift both of us from the ground seconds before the water that was swept away returns in a thunderous explosion.

Eudora, collapsed and burned beyond recognition, lies in the middle of the sand as water overtakes her remains. The flood of water returns to its home, covering everything that was visible moments earlier.

I set the lycanthrope on hard rock, and Nyssa rushes to his side. Other than her hair being slightly wet, she looks as beautiful as always.

"He's alive," she says, cradling him to her naked body. "He needs to shift to heal." She closes her eyes, calling on an invisible source, and begins rocking his wolf body with hers. Within seconds, the wolf disappears, returning to the lycanthropic human.

"Phyllis?" I ask.

"Over there," Nyssa nods with her head. Turning, I find the elderly witch collapsed. Her body is no larger than that of a child.

"Phyllis?" My words are soft as I turn her toward me. The skin on her face is sunken in, and dark circles underline her once vibrant eyes. Her heart is beating, but barely audible, even for me. Pulling her to my chest, I cradle the woman who quickly became my friend. "You did it. You helped keep the water away," I whisper. "We couldn't have done it without you. Eudora's dead."

Phyllis opens one eye and tries to smile. "Thank you for giving me something to live for. Save them...save the children, and get Thorne back." Soft heartbeats stop.

the wardrobe

I DON'T KNOW how much time passes before I let go of Phyllis's empty body. She would scold me for waiting so long, telling me that finding the children was more important than holding on.

"I'm sorry," Cam's weak voice says from behind. I turn, finding him leaning onto Nyssa as they overlook the woman that was once Phyllis.

"Me, too." I wipe a stray tear.

"I didn't know her long, but I don't think she'd want us standing around feeling sorry for her," Cam adds.

Nyssa kneels at the elderly witch's side. She lays a hand on her shoulder. "Elsie, put your hand on her other shoulder." I do as she asks, not sure what's about to happen. "Power bound, now unsealed, through blood and will, this bond we seal. From death's embrace to life renewed, let ancient strength find passage true."

With her words, white light rises from Phyllis's remains to my hand and into my body. "What just happened?" I ask, pulling away.

"Phyllis doesn't have anyone. She asked that if something were to happen to her, you receive her power."

"She did? Can all witches do that?" I kneel back to my friend.

"Some can, some can't. Phyllis could."

"I don't feel anything," I admit.

"Her energy is weakened. It will be there when you need it."

"We need to find the children," Cam says, calling us back to our mission.

Standing, I pull the map Brayden drew from my pocket. The once full sheet of paper is nothing more than shreds of fiber. "Shit, the map is destroyed by the water."

Cam turns to where the castle was earlier. "It's not like it would do any good anyway. There's nothing out here but rock and grass."

"They're here," I answer, moving to his side. "I can feel Alex."

"What about the others?" Nyssa asks.

I shake my head. "Just Alex. One of the girls, Everly, has the ability to hide energy. She may be shielding them."

"It's not going to take long to look." Cam stands straight. Nyssa reaches for him, offering strength. "I'm okay. I'm feeling much better."

"You two might want to find clothes."

"Clothes are the least of our worries," Cam answers. "Besides, we just fought a damn leviathan. Who cares what I'm wearing?"

"Phyllis would approve," I add with a smile. Cam laughs awkwardly.

"Yeah, she would."

"Do you still feel Alex's energy?" Nyssa asks.

"Aye. Just as strong as when we got here."

"Then they're here. If it was a facade, it would've disappeared when Eudora died." She nods toward me. "Follow your instincts."

"How the hell do I do that?"

"Stop thinking, and start feeling," Nyssa answers.

"I'm a fucking vampire. I don't feel anything."

"Tell Thorne and Phyllis that," she retorts.

I wipe a stray tear, acknowledging just how right she is. I close my eyes, pulling on the energy in my core. *Feel, don't think.* I repeat the words in my mind several times before opening my eyes. A slight shimmer flashes so quickly I'm not sure it wasn't my imagination. Staring in the same spot, I wait. I see it again, this time focusing my attention on what I'm seeing.

"Do you see that?" I whisper.

"What do you see?" Nyssa asks.

"Something...sparkled? I'm not sure that's the right

word." I start walking across the hard rocks, moving toward the invisible shimmer. Nyssa and Cam follow close behind. As we move, Alex's energy grows slightly. "It's stronger here."

"Keep moving toward the energy."

We walk until we can't walk any further. The three of us stand on the edge of a cliff overlooking the raging sea below. "You think they're in the water?" Cam asks.

I send my energy toward the sea below. Instantly, Alex's energy weakens. "He's not below us."

"That makes no sense." Cam scratches his head before motioning to the endless water in front of us. "They're not in the water, and there's no more land."

Nyssa moves to my side, staring into the open sea. "Eudora was the Goddess of the Sea. She could do anything she wanted."

Just as Nyssa speaks, the shimmer happens again. This time, lasting a few seconds longer. "Tell me one of you saw that."

"I did," Nyssa answers. She moves even closer to the cliff edge.

"Unless you can fly, Nyssa, which I wouldn't put past you, don't get too close," Cam warns.

Nyssa scoffs as her toes reach the ledge. She raises her hands high above her head, seemingly reaching toward the moon. "My energy is weakened. Elsie, lend me your power."

I move close to her side, placing an arm around her

waist. Closing my eyes, I pull through my core once more.

"Holy shit," Cam whispers.

I open my eyes as an illusion continues to dissolve. The endless sea and towering cliff face shimmer and ripple like a mirage in the heat. What emerges in their place is a small sea-weathered cottage, sitting as though it has been there the entire time, waiting to be found. "Holy shit," I echo.

"The children have to be inside." Cam steps forward. "I'm going first."

"Alex?" I call through my mind once more.

"Elsie?" his weak voice answers.

"We're coming!"

"Alex just answered me!" I shout to my friends. "He's weak."

Cam doesn't wait for more words. He steps onto the magical pathway with Nyssa and me on his heels. "Cam, be careful. I doubt they'll be sitting in the living room, watching television," Nyssa warns.

"They've likely been starved," I add. "You two might be more tempting than you realize."

"They're just kids," Cam says, showing his naivety about immortal children.

I pull him to a stop. "Cam. They may look and sound like children, but they're vampires who have most likely been starved for a while. Even weakened by hunger, they're going to be stronger than any vampire you've come in contact with before."

"Understood," he answers.

I step in front of him, leading the rest of the way to the cottage. To my surprise, the knob turns easily, and the door creaks open. Stepping into the cottage feels like stepping into another world. The air is warm, smelling like a mixture of sea salt and dried herbs. The interior is small but cozy, every detail crafted with enchantment.

On the far wall is a fireplace with a hearth that spans the entire width of the cottage. A fire cracks softly, casting shadows on the stone walls.

"Why does this place feel like Santa is going to come walking around the corner at any minute?" Cam whispers. "It even smells good in here."

"Alex? We're in the house. Where are you?"

"Elsie? Are you really here?" He sounds confused.

"Yes. We're here. Where are you?"

"It's dark..."

"Alex says it's dark where he is," I announce to Nyssa and Cam.

We split up, moving around the house, looking for a dark space large enough to hold three children. Within minutes, we've checked everywhere.

"What about this?" Nyssa says, standing in front of a ceiling-height wardrobe. She pulls at the locked door.

Cam steps in front of her, pulling on the door with no luck. "It's being held by something other than strength," he announces, stepping back.

"A spell," Nyssa says, moving in front of the wardrobe.

"How do we open it?" I ask.

"It depends on what spell she used."

"The goddess wouldn't use a spell to lock these doors. She has her own magic." I step away from the wardrobe. "It's made of wood."

Nyssa smiles, realizing what I'm saying. "Yes."

"What do you think...Oh, shit. Elsie, what if you hurt the kids?"

"They're vampires. They'll heal." I focus my attention on the wooden wardrobe and pull on my energy. "Burn," I whisper. Nothing happens. "Burn," I say again and again—nothing happens.

Nyssa puts her hand on my shoulder, reversing our earlier event. Energy floods me, filling me with power. "Again," she says.

I focus my attention on the large wardrobe. "Burn," I whisper. Flames begin immediately, lighting the top of the wardrobe on fire. "Burn," I repeat.

The wardrobe is fully engulfed minutes later, filling the cabin with smoke. Cam steps up, kicking the side of the large piece of furniture, knocking it on its back and to the floor. "That's enough," he says, coughing from the smoke.

Nyssa raises her hands, and a large gush of water diminishes the flames. I move to the doors and rip them off the hinges. The space is larger than the wardrobe should allow. The wooden panels inside are smooth and polished like glass. The air coming from inside is thick and musty-smelling.

The smoke clears, giving me a glimpse of what's inside. At first glance, the realm inside seems like a vast ethereal forest that stretches endlessly in every direction. Massive trees rise up, their trunks wrapped in thick vines.

"What is that?" Cam asks.

"Another world," Nyssa answers.

"Alex?" I call. "Everly? Autumn? It's Elsie! Where are you?" My voice echoes off the tall trees.

"We can't just wander through all of that," Cam announces the obvious. "They could be anywhere in that world."

"Alex!" I shout once again. "If you can hear me, come to my voice."

"It's dark," Alex's voice repeats.

"He says it's dark. That forest is not dark. Could they be somewhere else?" I ask.

"Not in the house." Nyssa climbs into the wardrobe. "Maybe this will work." Picking up a thick piece of bark, she slices it across the palm of her hand hard enough to break the skin and draw blood to the surface. Lifting her hand in the air, she chants a few words, and the wind picks up, blowing her hair and the surrounding trees. Cam and I flank her, ready for whatever is going to happen.

"That's brilliant. They'll smell you."

"Alex? Can you smell blood?"

"Yessss," he hisses. *"It smells delicious."*

"Break free of where you are, and follow the smell."

"He smells it," I warn Nyssa. "Be ready for anything."

I step next to my friend, not sure what's about to happen. "Something's coming," Nyssa whispers. "I feel it."

"Aye, me, too." I close my eyes, feeling Alex's energy growing stronger. Focusing my ears on every sound around me, I dial in on three distinct movements. "Both of you get out of here, now."

"I'm good," she argues.

"Now!" I turn, pushing her through the doors and back into the cottage. Cam follows close behind. It's then that I see them. The children I've dreamed of finding every day since they were taken. Everly, Autumn, and Alex stand several feet in front of me. Their once-clean clothes are torn and filthy. The looks on their faces have changed from innocence to killer.

"Elsie?" Autumn wrinkles her forehead.

"It's me," I answer, keeping my voice as calm as possible. "I'm here to take you home."

"We don't have a home," Everly answers, sniffing the air. "Where's the lycanthrope?"

"She's safe."

"We're hungry," Alex speaks for the first time.

"I know you are. I don't know how to help you."

"Let us have them," he retorts. "I smell two." For the first time in a long time, Alex scares me.

"I'm sorry it took so long to find you. We've been searching since Marnie took you."

"Marnie's gone," Autumn answers. "She went to a different realm."

I stare at the immortal child. "What? How do you know?"

She smiles, showing a mouth full of perfectly formed teeth. "I just do."

"Eudora's dead," I announce.

The children share a look. "How?" Everly asks.

"It's a long story that I'm happy to tell you one day. Today is not that day."

Alex sniffs the air once more. "Brayden?" he asks. "I smell him on you, but he smells—different."

I sigh, not sure how much to share. "Brayden's family was in an accident. He was the only one to survive, but barely."

"Celeste turned him into a vampire," he finishes my sentence. I forgot to shield my thoughts from the mind-reading child.

"Yes," I answer truthfully. "He helped us find you, find you all. He's ready to see you."

"You have no idea how you're going to get us off this island," he continues.

"Not yet. We didn't have much of a plan." I laugh, hoping to ease the tension.

"Who's Serafina?"

"She's a witch who has Thorne." I look into the eyes of the three children. "I promise to tell you everything once you've been fed and are stable. Now is not that time."

On cue, three bottles of blood are thrown through the doors, landing in front of me. The children have the bottles drained in the blink of an eye.

"More," Autumn says, and again, three more bottles are thrown inside. They drain them a little slower than the first. "More."

"That's enough," a young voice says from behind me. I turn, finding Brayden. He's wearing the same clothes as earlier and holding several more bottles of red liquid. "Hi, guys," he greets the immortal children.

"How?" I ask, not sure how he's here.

He shrugs. "I'm a good shield."

escape

"BRAYDEN?" Alex asks. "Is that really you?"

"It's me." Brayden smiles warmly. "We're here to get you off the island." I stare at the immortal child, unsure how he plans to accomplish his task. Hell, I don't even know how he got here.

"Who's we?" Autumn asks.

"Elsie, Cam, Nyssa, and Fran." Brayden waits for the information to sink in. "We need your help."

"Is that the only reason you came?" Everly asks.

"No," I interrupt. "We've been looking for you since the moment she took you. I've wanted nothing more than to find the three of you."

The children stare at me, making me uneasy. I'm not sure if they want to hug me or kill me. "Hug," Alex's voice says. "We want to hug you." His voice has returned to the kid who opened up to me, telling me the horrors of his life as he sat so small in a bathtub for the first time.

"I'd like that," I whisper and move in front of him.

"Elsie," Cam warns through the doors.

"He won't hurt me." I step into the child, wrapping my arms around his narrow waist and lifting him to me. Alex copies my movement as tiny arms close around my shoulders, and silent sobs begin.

"Thank you." A heartbeat later, two more sets of arms join the hug, wrapping around my thighs and hips. I can't control the tears that fall. I have no idea what they've been through, but from this moment on, I will protect them with my life.

"We have to go," Brayden says, interrupting the hugs. "Our window of time is about to pass."

"Meaning what?" Cam asks.

"Meaning high tide is fading. The island will disappear into another realm until the next tide. However, with Eudora gone, I'm not sure it will be able to return."

Brayden's words light a proverbial fire under my feet. I pull away, touching each child's cheeks. "You're safe. I promise. For now, we have to go. Do you understand?"

"Yes," they answer in unison.

"How are we leaving?" Nyssa asks.

"After we dropped you off, the jet landed on a nearby island. Fran chartered a local fisherman to bring us here."

"By chartered, you mean glamoured?" I interrupt.

"Same thing." He laughs. "Fran stayed with the boat to make sure he stayed 'glamoured.'"

I usher the immortal children through the destroyed doors of the wardrobe, through the cabin, and out into the night.

"It's over there," Brayden points to the edge of a cliff.

"We have to jump?" Cam asks, noticing the high edge. "That looks a little sketchy."

"It was the only place safe enough from the rocks for the boat."

The vampires arrive at the cliff before Nyssa and Cam. He was right. This jump would be sudden death for a human. Thankfully, we're not human. "Will you two be okay?" I ask, turning toward the lycan.

Nyssa raises her hands above her head and begins her now familiar dance. Under her command, the wind begins to blow, lifting her body from the terrain. "Hold on to me," she orders, reaching her hand toward Cam. He latches his hand through hers, and the two of them begin lowering gently to the awaiting boat.

"What is she?" Autumn asks, sniffing the air once more.

"That's another long story." I turn toward Brayden. "We're going to have to jump."

Everly lifts off the ground. "I'm going to fly."

I laugh awkwardly. "I forgot you borrowed that power from Kragen."

She offers her hands to the other children.

"Anyone want to come with me?" Brayden and Autumn accept her invitation, and the three of them lift off the ground, following Nyssa and Cam down the cliffside.

"I can't fly," I remind Alex. "I mean, I can, but I don't know how to control it, and I'd probably crash us into the side of the cliff."

Alex latches his fingers through mine, and the two of us jump, feet first, toward the raging water below. *"We're going to be okay,"* he says just as my feet hit liquid. *"Don't let go."*

My body is thrown around, slamming into rocks larger than a truck as I hold onto the small hand attached to mine. *"Alex, are you okay?"*

"I'm good. Swim toward the surface."

I kick, pulling the boy along with me. Just as we breach the water, a hand reaches down, grabbing the back of my shirt and pulling us to the side of a boat. "There you two are," Cam's deep voice says.

Turning sideways, I swing Alex's small body around, throwing him into the boat before I climb inside. He's on his feet, wringing water from the rags he's wearing, a heartbeat later.

"Thank goodness." Fran grabs all three immortal children in her arms, hugging them tightly. "I was so worried."

"We're okay," Everly answers.

"Good. Let's go home." Fran turns toward the boat captain, whose eyes are dilated abnormally large. "Take us back to the jet." The captain repeats her words before slowly backing away from the rocks.

The moon is still high and full as it shines on the island that once belonged to the Goddess of the Sea. "It's beautiful," Alex murmurs, leaning his entire weight on my side. "It didn't look like that where we were."

"What's happening to it?" Everly points at the rocks as they begin to disappear into the sea.

"The tide is receding, and the island is moving to another realm," Brayden answers.

"Thank you, Brayden. We couldn't have done this without you." I ruffle his now messy hair.

Turning toward the hybrid and lycanthrope in the back of the boat, I say, "I don't know how to thank either of you."

"You don't have to thank us," Nyssa answers for both of them.

The rest of the boat and plane ride is quiet. Other than a few soft whispers from the children, everyone spreads throughout the jet, focused on the trauma we've just experienced. Leaving Phyllis's body wasn't a choice I wanted to make, but there was no other option. My thoughts flash to her power moving into me after she passed. I don't even know what to do with my own power, let alone adding someone else's.

......

"Elsie?" Fran interrupts the silence of the plane ride. I raise my eyebrows in response. "Amelia says she's trying to text you."

I dig into my pocket, finding my phone. The screen is black and cracked, telling me it didn't survive the water. "It's dead." I wiggle the phone in the air.

"I don't really feel like talking. Can you take a message?"

"Clearly, you don't know Amelia very well." Fran stands, bringing her phone to me. "She wants to talk to you, not me. She's on the line."

Slowly, I put the phone to my ear. *"Hello?"*

"Fran tells me you have the kids."

"Yeah," I sigh with my words.

"That's awesome."

"Yeah. I'm sorry, Amelia. Is there something specific you want? I'm hungry, wet, and don't feel much like talking."

"You can't come back to New Orleans."

Shit. This again. *"Then we'll go to Charleston."*

"No. You can't go to Charleston either."

"Then where the hell can we land?" Alex glances my way. *"We're all hungry, and the kids need stability. We can't stay in the air the entire time."*

"The trance has gotten worse. More people are affected, including a few of Topher's strongest lycan."

"You said only the lycan who'd eaten raw meat recently were affected." I remind her of her words.

"That was the case. It's gotten worse. We can't find any

similarities between the victims other than they're from the paranormal community."

"What about the vampires? Are the only ones affected the ones who drink human blood?"

"So far, yes."

"It's Serafina," I admit. *"She bound them to her."*

"What the hell are you talking about, and who is Serafina?"

"Serafina is Thorne's half-sister, and she's a powerful witch. To be honest, that's an understatement. She's more than a witch."

"How is that even possible?" Amelia asks.

"A spell. A very powerful one."

"Fuck."

"I couldn't agree more." I pause, letting the information sink in. *"She has Thorne."*

"What do you mean, has him?"

"He's with her. She bound him to her." I fight the tears forming in my eyes.

"How? He doesn't drink human..."

"He did," I interrupt. The silence on the other end is deafening.

"I'm sorry, Elsie."

"Yeah, me, too."

"It's not safe to land." She reminds me.

I sigh. *"No one on board this plane has had human blood. The kids have been starved, only drinking the bottles of goat's blood Brayden brought them. The lycan haven't eaten anything except soup in a day, and everyone is exhausted. I'm going to have to override you and land this damn plane. The only way to stop her is to confront her. Running isn't going to help any of us or the ones she's bound."*

The pause on the other end of the line is deafening. I get the feeling it's been a while since anyone has disagreed with anything Amelia says. *"Okay,"* she answers finally. *"I understand. I'll tell the pilot to land in New Orleans."*

"No." I retort. *"We're going home. Thorne was last seen in Charleston. That's where we're going."*

"Okay." Her voice is heavy with concern. *"Elsie?"*

"Aye?"

"Be smart."

I take a deep breath before answering. I glance at the four immortal children who seem to be conversing telepathically. All four of them are killing machines, but right now, at this moment, they're nothing more than children. *"I'll try."*

"You made the right decision," Fran says, reaching for her phone. "Amelia doesn't see the whole picture. Serafina is the key."

"What about the grimoire?" Nyssa asks, moving closer.

"What grimoire?" Fran asks, looking between the two of us.

I close my eyes, not sure how to explain everything without a detailed flowchart, PowerPoint, and colored pencils. "My youngest brother, Aaron Abernathy, was a powerful warlock in Charleston. He left his grimoire for me."

Fran stares at me blankly. "Your youngest brother was a warlock and left *you* his grimoire?"

I nod. "Thorne gave the grimoire to Serafina."

"He did that because of being bound?" She fits the pieces of the puzzle together.

"We believe the reason Serafina performed the binding spell was to get to Aaron's grimoire," Nyssa adds.

Fran shakes her head. "If this woman is Thorne's half-sister, that would mean…"

"She's nearly three hundred years old." Cam fills in the blank, joining our group. "I don't get it either."

"Why didn't she take the grimoire while you were…"

"Aaron placed a spell on the book to open only under my hand. Blood of my blood, etc." I shrug, not sure I'm even saying it correctly.

"It was being guarded by our coven," Nyssa adds. "She tried to find it during the three hundred years without luck."

"What does she want with it?" Fran asks, looking between the three of us.

I look at my hands, remembering Phyllis's frail body I held hours earlier. "Aaron may have been working on a spell to siphon death."

Fran's forehead wrinkles. "Siphon death? Like zombies?"

Cam laughs. "Thank you. I had the same question." He runs a hand through his messy hair.

"A spell to siphon death from vampires. A spell to renew the life that was taken." I stare at Fran, waiting for her to fully grasp the insanity of my words.

"Holy shit," she whispers. "He wanted to use it on you."

"I think so."

"You believe Serafina is after this spell?"

Nyssa shrugs. "We don't know. Honestly, we don't know if he ever completed the spell."

"Serafina thinks he did," I answer.

"What is the purpose?" Fran asks. "What would be her reason for using the spell? A spell that would take immortality away, returning someone to human." She sighs.

"That is yet to be discovered."

"There have been times in my life that I would've given anything to be human again." Fran loses herself in thought. "Those times are gone. I would never wish this life on anyone, but at this point in my journey, I don't want to be human again."

"What about them?" Nyssa asks, nodding toward the kids.

"When Celeste sought spells to help her body grow, she sacrificed her immortality, yet still remains a vampire. If Aaron's spell can siphon death, they could live a normal *human* life." Fran's words are barely audible. Even as quiet as she was, I know each of the immortal children heard, although none responded.

"What are the chances that Serafina will be able to get into the grimoire and to Aaron's spell?" Fran asks.

"My guess is she's already trying. A spell, cast correctly, could get her inside." Nyssa wrings her hands as she speaks.

"Then it's only a matter of time," Fran adds.

"Aye."

"I'm in." Fran slides into the deep leather seat. "It's been a few months since I've experienced any real excitement."

"Us, too," Brayden says, standing from his seat.

"We need you," I answer, looking around the plane. "We need everyone."

"Then it's settled," Fran answers.

Several hours pass before we're on the ground in Charleston. To be honest, I have no clue where we were or how far of a flight it was. My mind has been reeling over possible scenarios and motives that Serafina might have for wanting Aaron's spell. I can't think of a single reason. She already has control of a huge majority of the paranormal community. What would be the purpose behind returning life to the vampires?

"I'll meet you back at the house," Cam says, interrupting my thought train.

"Me, too. I need a shower and some clothes that aren't someone else's." Nyssa motions down her body, showing the white bathrobe she discovered in the restroom of the plane.

"Understandable. We'll be there." I watch as the lycan hail a cab and disappear into the rising sun. The children and Fran follow me, walking at human speed until blending into the shadows. Once free of onlookers, we move faster than human eyes can track, stopping at the front door of the house Thorne and I rented together. His scent fills my nose, reminding me of what needs to be done.

"Fran, would you mind helping the children get cleaned up? I'm going to make a run to the store. They need clothes that will help them blend in."

"Sure." She smiles before turning to the quartet. "Let's go, everyone. It's time to wash the stink off and fill up your bellies."

"That's the best thing I've heard in a while," Alex says. He turns toward me as the rest of them move up the stairs. "Elsie?"

"Aye?"

"Thank you." Tears fill his small eyes. "I...I didn't think anyone would come."

I'm in front of him a heartbeat later. "I'm so sorry, Alex. I tried. *We* tried." I pull away, keeping my hands on his shoulders. "I never ever would've stopped until I found you."

"It was Brayden, wasn't it?"

"Aye. He knew how to find you."

Alex sniffs the air in front of me. "You smell different."

"You're not the only one who could use a shower." I laugh.

"No, you *smell* different." He sniffs once more. "You smell like—magic."

I stare, not sure how to respond. "Go get cleaned up. I'll be back soon." I watch the immortal child slowly work his way upstairs. Other than Thorne, Alex is the only person I've loved since becoming what I am. I fight to keep the tears from falling as the emotions overwhelm me.

"I love you, too," he says through my mind.

a means to an end

CAM AND NYSSA arrive together several hours after I return with clean clothes for the kids. They look exhausted, and Cam is sporting a few still-healing bruises, but they're here, and I'm grateful.

The kids have been upstairs since Fran held true to her promise of filling their bellies. They've been quiet, making me question what's going on. I've tried several times to tune into their conversation telepathically, but I'm either blocked or they're sitting in silence.

"Can we officially meet them?" Nyssa asks.

I shrug. "Sure." Looking upstairs, I call them through my mind. Within seconds, all four are standing at the top of the landing. In any other situation, seeing four immortal children vampires staring over an antique wooden banister would be terrifying. Honestly, it's a little terrifying right now. I scoff at the thought of being scared of a child. "Can you guys come down here?" In a heartbeat, all four are sitting on the couch, side by side. I take a deep breath, not sure what to say.

"I'm Autumn," the smallest of the four says. Her beautiful white-blonde hair is styled neatly in perfect braids, hanging down her side. "Mother turned me into a vampire in the 1950s."

"Mother?" Nyssa asks.

"It's a long story," I answer, remembering Patrice and her insanity.

"I can make things move just by thinking about it," Autumn continues.

"Telekinesis?" Cam asks. A large vase sitting next to him lifts off the table and slowly moves across the room, sitting on a table opposite where it started. "Pfft." He scoffs. "I'll take that as a yes."

The girl at the end waves. "Everly." Her thick curls are pulled tightly on top of her head in a thick bun. She looks at the other three children. "I guess Brayden and I are the newest. I was turned around twenty years ago." She wrinkles her tiny forehead. "I think...I've lost track of time."

"Do you have any abilities?" Cam asks.

"Yes and no." Everly looks at me with a questioning look on her face.

"Everly has the ability to borrow other people's abilities," I answer for her.

"Meaning what?" Nyssa asks.

"Meaning, I can borrow Autumn's ability to move things or Alex's ability to listen to people's minds," she points at Brayden, "or Brayden's ability to shield energies."

"Or fly," I add.

"Or fly." She giggles, reminding me of the innocent child she should be.

"That's amazing," Nyssa answers.

"Hi, I'm Alex," my favorite says with a coy wave. "I'm the oldest and the first. I was turned around a hundred years ago. Everly already told you my ability, but I can hear people's thoughts and talk to them in their minds."

"And, you know me," Brayden adds. "I'm the newest, and I have no idea what my abilities really are. I know things I shouldn't. I do things I don't know how to do." He shrugs. "I guess I'm a 'jack of all trades.'" His answer eases the tension in the room.

"I'm Nyssa." She smiles warmly.

"Cam." He waves.

"You smell like Topher," Alex says, directing his attention toward the lycanthrope.

"He's my brother. But don't hold that against me." Cam laughs loudly at his words. All four immortal children stare at him, void of emotion. He clears his throat and looks at the ground. The awkwardness that flows from him makes me smile.

"Why would we hold that against you?" Alex says.

"I...I don't know. It's just a saying. I didn't mean anything by it."

Alex's smile is infectious. "I'm just messing with you, Cam. We know what it means. I'm sorry."

Cam's smile mimics Alex's. "You had me for a minute." He runs a hand through his hair. His words and body language don't match. He's still uneasy around the kids, making me wonder if it's a Cam thing or if he senses something I don't.

Brayden slides forward on the couch. "Nyssa? I've been doing a bit of research while we were upstairs, and I hope you don't mind me bringing up your heritage in front of the others."

She shakes her head. "Of course not."

"There isn't much written on druids other than lore and ideological concepts. Can you tell me how you discovered your heritage?"

Nyssa slides back in her seat, crossing her long legs at the knees. "In my case, I always knew who I was. My mother was the last of her kind, a full-blooded druid, and taught me the truth of who I was from early childhood."

"But she wasn't the last, was she?" he continues.

Nyssa leans forward, making eye contact with the immortal child. "Clearly, she wasn't. The druid blood runs through your veins."

"What does it mean for me?" he asks. The two of them stare at each other so intently, it's as if they're alone in the room.

"I don't know what it means for you," Nyssa says.

"Like me, you are the only one of your kind. We are hybrids. Half killer, half harmonizer."

"Harmonizer?" he repeats, wrinkling his forehead. "I haven't heard that term before."

"A druid's responsibility is to balance the natural world, along with the spiritual realms, and our own powers to maintain harmony in all things. Unlike me, you are eternal. Being a vampire, your life will continue long after mine is over. Your effect on the harmony of the world will be much greater than mine."

"Wow," Autumn whispers. "That's kind of cool."

"Will you help me? Help me to learn how to *harmonize*?" Brayden asks.

"Of course." Nyssa smiles with her answer. "I'd be honored."

Several minutes of awkward silence pass before Alex asks the question I've been waiting for since returning. "Who's Serafina?"

I take a deep breath, not sure how to explain everything that's happened. "Serafina is a powerful witch. She and my brother were friends."

"You have a brother that's still alive?" Everly asks. "Is he a vampire?"

"No. He died two hundred and fifty years ago."

"I'm confused how that works," Autumn announces, looking around the room.

I huff a laugh. "He was a warlock who lived here, in Charleston, during the early 1700s. Serafina was alive during the same time. She cast a spell that's kept her alive since then."

"Spells can do that?"

"That and more," Nyssa answers.

"Serafina was—*is* very powerful. Not long after coming to Charleston, she crafted a spell to bind paranormal creatures to her," I continue. "She recently cast that spell."

"Paranormal creatures? Like vampires?" Alex asks.

"And lycan and some witches. However, the only ones she's managed to bind to her so far are vampires who drink human blood and lycan who've eaten raw meat recently, although that seems to be changing."

"Thorne doesn't drink human blood," Alex interrupts.

"Normally, no." I don't go into detail.

"So, this woman, who was friends with your brother, bound Thorne to her?" Autumn asks. "Why?"

"Control," Fran answers. "It's what most people want. It gives them a sense of purpose. A sense of power."

"Because he was bound to her, Thorne went with Serafina willingly. He took a very important piece of the puzzle with him." I find a particularly worn area of the floor to focus my attention on. "My brother's grimoire."

"What's a grimoire?" Everly asks.

"A magical book of spells, rituals, and knowledge," Nyssa answers. "Most witches and warlocks own them. They're usually passed down through families."

"She wants the spell your brother crafted to siphon death." Brayden gets straight to the point.

"Siphon death? Am I the only one who doesn't know what that means?" Everly asks.

"My brother, Aaron, was an infant when I was taken. He didn't remember me but knew I was taken by vampires. I don't know all the details, but I'd imagine after years of stories, he decided to take action. He created a spell that would siphon death from me, making me human again." The children stare blankly at me, seemingly absorbing my words.

"Could we become human again?" Brayden asks.

"Theoretically, yes. You could be human again." My voice is no louder than a whisper.

The immortal children become quiet, no doubt having a silent conversation that they've managed to exclude the rest of us from.

"The only way to prevent the spell from being cast is to stop Serafina," Nyssa says, staring at the children. "She's going to get into that grimoire. When she does, she won't hesitate to use it." Nyssa's words are directed toward the immortal children. Whatever silent conversation they were holding wasn't as private as they believed.

"You don't want to be human?" I ask, connecting the dots.

"No," they answer in unison.

"Even if it means you'll stay a child for eternity?"

They look at each other before answering. "We

won't be children forever. Celeste is going to help us grow."

Autumn raises her tiny hand in the air. "Why does Serafina want a spell that will siphon death? If the vampires are already under her control, why would she want to kill them...or unkill them?"

"Maybe she just doesn't like vampires," Cam answers.

"We don't know," I answer truthfully. "One thing I've learned throughout my life is that it's not always our time to discover why. To the world, her reasoning may be something unimportant. To her, it may be everything. Our role is to prevent Serafina from casting the spell."

"Where do we start?" Brayden asks.

"That's an excellent question," I answer. "We have no way of knowing where they've gone."

"Can't you track Thorne?" Everly asks.

"No. We don't share blood. I can hear him telepathically and feel his energy when we're near each other, but I've never been able to track him. He's bound to Serafina. He's not going to answer, even if he's next door."

"I was able to track him in New Orleans," Alex interrupts.

"Aye, you were, but this is different. He's...he's different now." I don't go into detail.

"What about a spell? Could a spell find him?" Alex directs his question toward Nyssa.

She stands, walking across the large room. "A location spell works in the human world or even on a lycanthrope. But a vampire is different. Warm blood doesn't flow through his body." She looks down before continuing. "His soul is...cold." I've never heard a vampire described that way. Is my soul cold? Do vampires have a soul?

"What about the grimoire?" Everly asks. "If it belonged to Elsie's brother, could it emanate an energy that only Elsie could pick up on?"

"Holy shit, Everly. Why didn't I think of that?" Nyssa turns toward me. "The grimoire was tuned to your energy. That's how you were able to open it in the first place. That means it will still be tuned to your energy."

"Okay. Tell me what that means."

"It means Everly is right. You can find the grimoire, which will lead us to Serafina..."

"And Thorne," I interrupt.

"And Thorne," she confirms.

"It's not going to be that easy," Fran says. "I'm sorry to be the party pooper, but Serafina is smart. Don't you think she would've already planned for that? Yes, Elsie is connected to the grimoire, but couldn't Serafina just cast a spell to prevent the energy from finding its way back here?"

"A druid could find them," Brayden says quietly.

"I appreciate the ego boost, but I'm no stronger than my spells," Nyssa counters.

"What I witnessed you do on Eudora's island was no spell. You transformed into a whale. The ocean waves and moon danced to your will. That was all you, Nyssa. That was raw, unfiltered power." I stare at my new friend. "Brayden's right. You can find them."

She sighs, clearly exasperated by our suggestion. "I've spent my entire life hiding that part of me. If I'm honest, I don't know how I did what I did back there. It just happened. Even if I do manage to find them, I'm not strong enough to fight them. I'm no match for Serafina's power, and from what I felt flow into Thorne during the ceremony, he's..." She stops, staring into my eyes.

"He's what?" I ask, not sure how to interpret her words.

"He's like me." She nods at Brayden. "Like him."

"Thorne is a druid?" Brayden asks.

Nyssa nods. "I think so. It's the only thing that makes sense."

I stare at Nyssa, not sure if I understood her words correctly. "You think Thorne has druid blood?"

"Yes."

"What about Serafina?" Cam asks. "If they share the same father, wouldn't they share the same bloodline?"

"No," Nyssa answers. "Druid abilities are traditionally passed through the matriarchal line. Thorne received his druid abilities from his mother. Serafina most likely inherited her magical abilities from *her* mother, meaning they don't share the same magical abilities."

Cam looks around the room. "Is anyone else wondering what the hell was wrong with their dad? He had a type, didn't he?"

"Apparently," Autumn answers, making me smile.

"If Thorne has druid blood, we should be able to find him." Brayden stands, moving closer to Nyssa. "His ancestry will call to ours."

"What makes you say that?" Nyssa asks. "I sensed the power inside you, but it didn't *call* to me."

His tiny shoulders rise. "I just know."

"Then it's settled. While you two figure out how to locate Thorne, the rest of us will figure out how to kill Serafina." I stand, leaving the group in the room.

a boy and his powers

I SIT on the perfectly made bed in the bedroom that Thorne and I claimed when we came here. His clothes are still hung in the closet, along with his hygiene items. He didn't take anything other than the clothes on his back.

There has to be a way to counter the binding spell. If we manage to kill Serafina, will the spell die with her? I make a mental note to ask the only remaining witch in the house. A knock on the door draws me back to reality.

"Elsie," Alex's soft voice says from behind the closed door.

"Aye."

"May I come in?"

"Of course." Unlocking the door, I open it to see large brown eyes staring back at me. "Is everything okay?"

He shrugs. "I think so. Brayden and Nyssa talked briefly, and now they're telekinetically moving things around the house."

"That sounds fun." I laugh as Alex moves across the wide planks, sitting on the edge of the four-poster bed. "But I meant you. Is everything okay with you?" His energy feels different.

"What do you know about Serafina?" he asks.

"Not much," I admit. "She's from Scotland, apparently had a 'fling' with my baby brother," I shudder at the thought, "and is so powerful she was able to trick Thorne and me, making us believe we had traveled to New Orleans and Brayden."

Alex's eyes grow several sizes. "How is that even possible?"

I shrug. "She was able to cast an illusion grand enough to make us think we flew on a plane to Louisiana, went to Fran's house, and had an entire conversation with Brayden. I realize how insane that sounds, but yeah...she did that."

"Are you sure she's a witch?"

I think back to Phyllis's description of the three-hundred-year-old sorcerer. "I was told she was a witch. I have no reason not to believe the person who told me."

Alex stares at me without speaking. I know without asking, he just read my thoughts on Phyllis. "I'm sorry," he whispers. "I know I shouldn't read your thoughts." He picks at a loose thread on the chenille bedspread. "Your shield is *easier* to get through than before."

"I'm not using it," I admit.

"*Why not?*" he asks through my mind.

"*I have nothing to hide from you. But I'd be remiss if I didn't remind you that listening to someone's thoughts...*"

"I know. It's rude," he repeats my words from earlier. "I missed you, Elsie."

Touching his arm, I rub my thumb across his smooth skin. "I missed you, too, Alex. I'm glad you're back."

"Thank you for coming for us." He plays with the loose thread again.

"I'm sorry it took so long."

He shakes his tiny head. "Don't apologize." Turning his head, he wipes a tear. "I've never had anyone who would've come after me. You're the first person who...the first person who didn't lie or hurt me."

I move in the blink of an eye, wrapping my arms around him. "I'm here. I'll be here as long as you want me."

"Always," he whispers. "I'll want you to be here, always." He stays in my arms until his tears dry. Growing up the oldest of nine, I was the fill-in mother for my younger siblings. After Kragen took me, turning me into a vampire, being a mother wasn't something I ever allowed myself to think about. The love I feel towards this tiny immortal child brings out the protective mother that's been hidden away for three centuries.

"I'm not going anywhere," I whisper back.

"Elsie, Alex?" Autumn's soft voice says from the hallway. "Can I come in?"

Alex pulls away, drying his tear-stained face, and nods. "Sure," I answer. The tiny blonde enters the room with a worried look on her face. Her clothes are soaking wet, and water drips from the ends of her braids. "What's up?" I ask, hoping to lead into the reason she's soaking wet.

She sighs. "It's Everly."

"Okay?"

"She's acting weird."

"Acting weird, how?" Alex asks, sliding off the bed.

"Well...she just flooded the room we were sharing."

I stare at the immortal child, not sure how to respond. "Did she leave the sink or bathtub running?" Nothing else makes sense.

Her tiny head shakes from side to side. "No. She just did it."

"With her mind?" Alex asks.

"Yeah. We were talking about Eudora, and the room suddenly flooded."

Alex looks at me. "Is it possible for her to borrow a goddess's power?"

I laugh loudly. "I've learned that with you three, anything is possible." I jump off the bed, joining Alex and Autumn. "We might need to get a mop."

The three of us pass Nyssa and Brayden, staring intently at each other in the living area. I can't hear their silent conversation, but I have no doubt that's what's happening. Cam's asleep in the chair next to them, completely unaware of anyone else in the room.

"What's going on?" Brayden asks, pulling his gaze away from Nyssa.

"Everly stole Eudora's power and flooded the room," Autumn announces like it's an ordinary occurrence.

"What?" Nyssa asks, wrinkling her forehead. "Her abilities were able to mimic a goddess's?"

"That's what we're on our way to find out," I answer, moving through the room.

"Can we come?" Brayden asks, standing. I don't answer as he and Nyssa join our small group, moving toward the flooded room.

Autumn is right. My feet smack against a few inches of water covering the antique wooden floors of the second-floor hallway. I lead the group into the room, finding Everly on her hands and knees with a pile of wet towels behind her. "Everly, is everything okay?"

The immortal child rocks back on her thighs and wipes tears from her tear-stained face. "Elsie, I'm so sorry. I don't know what happened. It just came out of nowhere."

"It's okay, sweetie. These things happen. Well...they don't happen very often, but they happen."

My words do nothing to ease her frustration. Everly

sniffs loudly, wiping her runny nose on her sleeve. "I'll go to the basement," she says, standing.

"What in the hell happened here?" Fran asks, coming into the room.

"I flooded it," Everly admits. She wipes her eyes again, moving past the group into the hallway.

"Everly? Why are you going to the basement?" I ask as she passes.

"It's where Mother would send us for punishment," Autumn answers for her sister. "It's where she would..." She doesn't finish her sentence.

Everly moves slowly down the hallway, making squishing sounds as she moves. "I'm not going to punish you, Everly."

The immortal child stops, turning her tiny head in our direction. "But I flooded the room."

In the time I've known the children, I've never thought of them as children until now. Whatever Patrice did to them, I don't want to think about. I move in front of the soaking-wet vampire and wrap my arms around her. "I am not Mother. You're safe here."

Quiet tears turn into loud sobs as Everly rests her head on my stomach. "I'm sorry, Elsie."

I pull her to arm's length, looking into her deep brown eyes. "Do you know how amazing you are? You flooded a room with no access to water using only your mind. That's something to be celebrated, not punished. You borrowed a goddess's power."

Everly sniffs loudly. "You really think so?"

"Um, yes."

"But the room is ruined. The floors, the carpet..."

"I can fix that," Nyssa interrupts. She steps into the room, and the energy surrounding us changes instantly. "Earth below and sky above, balance water, take what's enough. Air, rise and carry away, leave this space dry today." I watch in awe as the druid lifts her arms to her side, rotating them slowly throughout the room. With her movements, the water begins to dissipate. Seconds later, the once-flooded bedroom is dry with no signs of ever being flooded.

"How did you do that?" Brayden asks.

"The elements helped me."

Everly walks back to the room. "Thank you."

"You're welcome, little one." She ruffles the curls on Everly's head. "If you can harvest the power of Eudora, you are going to be a huge asset in this fight."

"The children shouldn't have to fight." Fran has her arms across her chest defiantly.

"I agree," I add.

"I want to fight," Brayden interrupts. He looks at the other three immortal children. "We all want to fight. We've discussed it."

"Serafina isn't Eudora. With the goddess, we knew what we were up against. With Serafina, we don't have any idea of what she's capable of," I argue. "She's bound vampires and lycan to her, which gives her even more power. I won't allow you four to risk your lives."

Autumn moves in front of me. "With all due respect, Elsie, you don't get to make that decision for us. We may look like children, and to the world around us, we are children, but we're not ordinary. We're vampires. We have abilities that would be useful for whatever the witch wants to throw at us."

"Autumn, I know you think you're strong, but..." My words stop short as the antique four-poster bed lifts from the floor several feet into the air. The tiny vampire turns her head toward a solid wood dresser. I watch as it lifts off the ground, completely spinning in the air.

Autumn crosses her arms in front of her chest and yawns. "Should I continue? I could do this all day."

"What the hell did I miss?" Cam asks, coming into the room. "That was one hell of a nap."

"Elsie doesn't want us to fight, and Everly stole Eudora's power and flooded the room," Alex answers for the group.

"That helps," Cam answers sarcastically.

Alex and Everly move to Autumn's sides as she sets the large pieces of furniture back in place. "I know you're trying to protect us, Elsie. We don't need protecting." Alex's words are soft. "We can do this."

"What if..." The room transforms into the bowels of Kragen's ship before I complete my sentence. The smell of death slaps me in the face. It's a smell I will remember for as long as I walk the earth. "Alex? Fran? Brayden?" What just happened? Serafina? I look around the room, allowing my vampire eyes to focus on the familiar details of the room. Rotting flesh covers the floor, while the rats that sustained my life for a century scurry throughout their remains.

The roar of the ocean, lapping against the bow of the ship, threatens to turn me into the lost girl being held captive once again. "This isn't real," I say out loud. I close my eyes, willing the image to disappear, returning me to the house in Charleston.

My eyes open to the familiarity of the ship. "This isn't real," I repeat. This time, my words sound frantic, even to me. "This isn't real. This isn't real. This isn't real."

"It's real," a familiar voice says from behind. I turn, finding Brayden. He's dressed in the same clothes that I bought him earlier.

"Brayden? How are you here? How am I here?"

He shrugs. "I read your mind."

"Why here?"

"I needed you to know how powerful we are." Large blue eyes stare into mine. "Alex, Autumn, Everly, and I are the only ones strong enough to overcome her. Plus, she has Thorne's power under her control right now."

"What are you saying, Brayden?"

"I'm saying you're going to die if you don't let us help you. Thorne will die. Fran will die. Nyssa and Cam will die..."

"Okay, I get it," I interrupt. "How did you do this?"

Brayden takes a deep breath. "I don't know." He

kicks a huge rat across the uneven floorboards. "I've seen it in your mind several times."

"Seen what?"

"This." He motions around the room where I was held captive.

"Brayden? Can you see images in my mind?"

He shrugs. "Sometimes. Only when you're focused or really sad. I have to concentrate hard to see it."

"Did you use a spell?" I ask, not sure how he has the same ability Serafina does.

"No. I just pictured it in my head with us standing here." He lowers his head. "I'm sorry, Elsie. I can see how horrible this place was. I don't know why I brought you here."

"It was horrible, but I'm not sorry you brought me here."

He looks up, smiling slightly. "I thought you were angry at me."

"Angry, no. Annoyed, yes." I move closer to the young boy. "You're right. We can't defeat her and get Thorne back without you. Without *all* of you."

Brayden's arms wrap around my waist. "Thank you."

"I had no idea you could do this."

"Me, neither." He laughs.

"Can you do it again?"

"I think so. It was easy. Why?"

I clap my hands, echoing through the wooden ship. "This is how we're going to fight and win."

"On a ship?"

"No. In the world that *we* create," I answer. "It's the only way."

"I don't understand."

"Aye. Me, neither—yet. Take us home, Brayden. We've got a plan to create."

the magic of illusion

AS QUICKLY AS the illusion appeared, it vanished, returning me to the once-flooded bedroom in Charleston. The mixture of paranormal creatures stares at me expectantly.

"Elsie?" Fran asks. "Did something happen?"

"How long was I gone?" I ask.

"Gone? You've been right here the entire time." Alex touches my elbow.

"That's not true, is it, Brayden?"

The apprehensive look on his face tells me he's not sure how to answer. "Technically, yes. But, mentally, no."

"What the hell does that mean?" Fran asks.

Moving toward the bed, I sit on the edge of the thick mattress. "One moment, I was here, talking to everyone, and the next, I was transported to Kragen's ship."

"But he's dead," Autumn announces.

"Aye, he is. Brayden created an illusion to make me think I was on the ship."

Every eye in the room turns toward the immortal child. "Brayden created an illusion?" Cam repeats my words slowly. "How?"

The young child shrugs, looking more like an eight-year-old than ever. "I saw it in my mind, and it happened."

"He has the power of illusion," Nyssa adds. "That is rare."

"We can use it against her." I look into the eyes of my new friends. "Don't you see?"

"No," Fran answers for the group.

"Brayden can use his ability to bypass Serafina's illusions by creating illusions of his own, like creating a world inside of a world." My words sound confusing even to me.

"You're saying that Brayden creates a world inside of Serafina's world?" Cam asks.

"That's exactly what I just said."

"It's not going to be that easy," Nyssa answers. "What if she creates a world where he's not able to use his ability? Or separates us from one another? Or..."

"I could communicate with everyone," Alex answers. "I can hear everyone's thoughts and could keep us in one spot or at least one mind."

"Me, too," Everly adds. "I just have to borrow Alex's ability."

"Elsie, you just said you didn't want the kids

involved. Now, you're planning a war based on their powers." Fran crosses her arms protectively over her chest. "You can't ask that of them."

"She's not," all four answer in unison.

"Shit, that was like a moment from *The Shining*," Cam says, bringing a smile to my face. "How did y'all do that?"

"We want to help," Everly answers.

"We're *going* to help," Alex adds.

"You can't do it without us, and we're not taking no for an answer." Brayden refuses to back down.

"I know," I whisper. I turn toward Fran. "Believe me, it's hard to put them in danger, but they're not human. They're powerful vampires with abilities that can change the world."

"Okay." Fran's words don't match the look on her face. "If something happens to one of you, I'm going to be pissed." The immortal children share a laugh, easing the tension in the room.

"I'll be the first one to agree that we needed to recoup and rest, but we've been here long enough. The longer we wait, the stronger Serafina will become, along with the binding spell. We're on limited time." Nyssa looks around the group as she speaks. "I don't think she's going to be able to cast a spell that will open the grimoire. When she realizes that, she's going to come for Elsie, either physically or spiritually through a spell."

"How long will that take?" Alex asks, moving protectively to my side.

Nyssa shrugs. "I don't know. But my gut says not long."

"Is Elsie the only one able to open the grimoire?" Fran asks.

"Most likely. However, Serafina is strong. If anyone could open it, it would be her. It comes down to the strength of Aaron's magic when he placed the spell."

"Then we can't wait," Brayden answers. "We can't sit around here, waiting for her to show up or cast a new spell. We have to go to her."

"That's all well and good, but you're all forgetting something. We have no idea where she is or where to look." Cam is the voice of reason.

"There has to be a way to find her. Can you create a spell or something? Maybe connect to the elements?" Everly asks Nyssa.

"If Serafina were human or even a lesser witch, yes. But her magic is powerful and guarded. Even my abilities can't break through."

"What about someone who is bound to her? Would they know how to find her?" Cam asks.

Nyssa shrugs. "Maybe?"

"Maybe doesn't help," Fran answers.

"Maybe it's better than nothing. Excuse me for a moment." Cam pulls a cell phone from his pocket and steps into the hallway.

"Even if a bound vampire or lycan could connect us to her, how would we find one?" Nyssa asks.

"What about the flight attendant? Terri?" I ask. "She had the symbol on her neck that Amelia warned me about."

"Got it taken care of," Cam says, coming back into the room. He slides his phone back into his pocket. "Connor is sending a bound vampire to us within the hour. Apparently, he and my brother, Topher, have been in contact throughout all this. Connor trapped one of Serafina's vampires."

"Someone's bringing the vampire here?" Nyssa asks.

"No. I'm meeting them downtown. The vampire has been wrapped in silver and is being *subdued*."

"Can I come?" Brayden asks. "It will give me a chance to practice illusions."

"That's a good idea." I make eye contact with everyone in the room. "If we're going to do this together, I think we should all go."

"Agreed," Fran and Nyssa answer in unison.

"This sounds like fun," Alex says. For the first time since meeting the stoic immortal child vampire, he uses sarcasm.

Thirty minutes later, Cam pulls Phyllis's SUV to a stop in front of a familiar bar. "They have the vampire here?" I ask.

"If you're going to hold a vampire hostage, there's

no place better to do it than the lycan headquarters." Cam's words make more sense than I care to admit.

Every eye turns toward us as we enter. Several older men at a round table in the back growl deeply, lifting their noses into the air. "Damn bloodsuckers," one of them mumbles.

"Elsie?" Alex calls through my mind. *"Are we sure this is smart?"*

"No," I answer truthfully.

Following Cam into the Alpha of Charleston's office, the smell is the first thing that I notice. Where Connor's office usually smells like a wet dog, today, the soft smell of copper fills my senses. Autumn looks at me and wrinkles her nose, no doubt, smelling the same odor.

Connor stands from his desk, moving in front of me. His large arms wrap around my back, pulling me to his chest. I don't know what I expected, but a bear hug wasn't it.

"It's good to see you, Elsie." He pulls away, keeping his hands on my shoulders. "I'm sorry about Thorne."

"Aye, me, too. We're going to get him back."

Connor stares at me for a few silent seconds before agreeing. "Yeah, we are."

"Where's the vampire?" Nyssa interrupts.

For the first time since entering, Connor takes inventory of the group that followed me through the door, pausing at Nyssa. "I'm sorry. Who are you?"

"Nyssa Jamison," she answers, offering her hand.

He shakes it, staring into her dark eyes longer than needed.

"Hello, Nyssa Jamison. Connor McFadden, Alpha of Charleston. It's a pleasure to meet you. You're not in a pack?" His words are more of a statement than a question.

"I'm not," Nyssa answers with a smile.

"You're the Alpha?" Brayden asks.

"I am." Connor sniffs the air. "You're the new one?"

Brayden snickers at his comment. "I am." He moves closer to the Alpha. "We're here to see the vampire."

"I figured as much," the Alpha answers. He leans against the corner of his thick wooden desk, crossing wide, muscular arms in front of him. "She's in the back."

"She?" I ask. I assumed the vampire was male. I have no idea why.

"Her name is Arina. She was caught after she...after she murdered two of my strongest lycan."

"Shit," Cam murmurs.

"She's strong, stronger than she should be," Connor continues.

"Has she said anything?" Fran speaks for the first time.

"Other than hurling insults and nearly breaking free of her chains several times, no."

I stare at the Alpha, not sure I heard him correctly. "She broke through the silver?"

"Yes."

The look on Fran's face mimics my thoughts. Whoever Arina is, she's strong. Silver weakens even the strongest. Connor's eyes look tired. "Three of you can go in."

"With all due respect, Connor. We're all going to be included in this mission. It's going to take all of us to get the information we need." Nyssa's voice is calm, making me wonder if she's working some sort of spell on the Alpha.

"Okay," Connor agrees. "Cam and I will join you." He looks at the immortal children. "What about the kids?"

"We'll be fine," Everly answers for the group.

Connor sighs. "Follow me."

He leads us back through the main bar and through a door on the other side of the building. The further we move, the stronger the vampire energy becomes. I felt it when we arrived, but now, it's nearly overpowering. Connor stops at a heavy door wrapped in silver chains. "This room is used for lycan who have *trouble* with the shift." He slides on a pair of thick rubber gloves before unlocking what looks like a logging chain wrapped around the handles. "Don't listen to her bullshit," he warns, pulling the heavy door open and lighting an ancient torch next to the door.

The room is small and lined with heavy steel bars. Tied against the far wall is Arina, Serafina's bound vampire.

"Who have you brought me, wolf?" she asks as we

move into the room. Her accent is sharp and clipped, reminding me of the time I spent in India while running from Kragen. Arina locks eyes with me, then Fran, before noticing the others.

"I'm Elsbeth," I answer.

"Fran." She doesn't elaborate.

"You have children?" the vampire asks.

"Where are you from?" I ask, ignoring her question.

"Tsk, tsk, tsk. You first."

"They're not mine," I answer, evading a direct answer.

"She has an ability," Brayden says through my mind. Arina smiles knowingly.

"Shield up," I say to anyone listening. "Your turn to answer." I remind the bound vampire.

"Nepal," she answers. "Originally."

"How did you end up here?" Nyssa asks.

"I don't speak to witches."

"How did you end up here?" Fran repeats the question without missing a beat.

Arina rolls her eyes. "I assume you mean America, not in this cell." She smiles, making me sick to my stomach. "It's a long story that I am not inclined to share." She sniffs the air once more. "Has being around these...children weakened you that much?"

"I am not weak."

"Kragen is her maker," Everly says through my mind. In an instant, his smell hits me.

Arina smiles knowingly. "Now you know. *He* brought me here. He brought us both here."

I stare at the vampire, not sure what to say. We share the same maker, Kragen, the asshole. We are sisters in a weird fucked-up way. "I killed him."

"I know," she whispers several minutes later. "Thank you."

"Do you know why we're here?" I ask, moving the conversation away from Kragen.

"This." She turns her head sideways, showing the moon behind her ear.

"How do you know Serafina?" Fran asks.

Arina smiles. "I don't know who you're talking about."

"She's lying," Everly says, not even bothering to speak telepathically. "She's been there, to her home."

"What do we have here?" Arina asks, looking at Everly.

"Tell us where Serafina is," the immortal child continues.

"You're nothing more than a child. Why would I betray the one who loves me for you?"

"Did Kragen love you?" I interrupt. Arina turns her attention back toward me. "Did he force you to become a vampire?"

"Kragen was my maker. That is all." For a brief moment, the shield that she's obviously had in place since we walked in lowers, showing me a glimpse of a familiar pirate ship.

"Brayden?" I ask, hoping he saw the same glimpse I did.

A heartbeat later, I'm standing in the bowels of Kragen's ship. Next to me is Brayden, and chained against the wall is Arina. She's in the same spot where I spent a century, held in place with silver, just like I remember.

"What is this?" she asks, looking around the dark room. "Where am I?"

"I think you know," I answer.

"This isn't real," she retorts. "This is the witch."

I move closer to the beautiful vampire. "Do you see the witch anywhere around? It's just them and us." I point at the pile of rotten body parts. Pieces of what used to be humans are discarded and used for food.

"This is where he kept you." I step even closer. "Did you enjoy drinking from the rats?" Arina doesn't answer, but from the look on her face, I've struck a chord. "Did he drag you behind the ship for weeks at a time when it was *bathtime*?"

"Shut up," she spews. "You don't know what you're talking about."

I send an image of Kragen, the sound of his keys rattling against the lock on the door, the smell of the mixture of sea air and blood that followed him everywhere. Every dark memory I've worked so hard to forget, I send to Brayden in one thought.

Chill bumps cover my skin as Kragen's keys rattle

on his way down the stairs. "He's here," I whisper to Arina.

"How are you doing this?" she repeats.

The lock clinks as the heavy wooden door slides open. "There you are, my dear. I thought you might be *out.*"

"He can't see us," Brayden says through my mind.

Kragen moves closer to Arina without acknowledging Brayden or me. "I believe it's time for you to do what I made you to do."

"No," Arina whispers as Kragen reaches down, unlocking the chain around her waist. He leans over, sinking his teeth into her chest. Instinctively, I cover Brayden's eyes.

"She'll kill me," Arina says as Kragen pulls his teeth out of her skin.

"Don't be silly, whore. You're already dead." Kragen wraps his arm around her wrist, pulling her to her feet. "I may have my way with you first." He slaps her across the face with the back of his hand, pushing her back a few feet.

"No," she says, standing to her feet. "You're dead. This isn't real."

"This is very real." He grabs her, pulling her toward the door.

"Stop this," she pleads, turning toward Brayden and me.

"Where is Serafina?" I ask.

Kragen turns back, raising his hand to her once

more. "Slap me again, and I will kill you where you stand." Arina's words are low and calculated.

The pirate smiles as he slams his hand against her cheek once more, this time the force throwing her on top of a pile of body parts. He reaches down, yanking a handful of dark hair from her head. "Get up, bitch."

We follow as he drags her out of the bowels of the ship, up familiar stairs, and to the stern. "She needs a bath," he shouts toward a deckhand.

"No." She begins to cry. "Don't do this."

"We can make it go away," I whisper. "Tell us where to find Serafina."

"I'll tell you what you want to know. I'll tell you where to find her. Get me out of here." Tear stains cover her cheeks as she begs me for freedom. The facade quickly fades, returning us to the steel-barred room. The stoic woman from before is gone, replaced by someone far more familiar than I'd like to admit.

this sucks...

"WHAT JUST HAPPENED?" Fran asks, looking between the three of us.

"Arina has had a change of attitude," I answer without truly answering.

"Where is Serafina?" Brayden asks, ignoring the group around us.

Arina sighs. "Where she always is, the——" The vampire's mouth is open, still trying to speak, while her words are silenced. She tries again, opening her mouth, while what looks like an invisible vice holds her words. "What the hell?" she asks out loud.

"We don't have time for games, Arina," I warn.

"I'm not playing any games." She takes a deep breath. "Serafina is at——"

"Brayden? It seems it's bath time." He nods, understanding my words.

"No! I'm not playing any games. I swear. I'm trying to tell you, but the words won't come out!" She coughs several times loudly, making more of a scene than before. She takes a deep breath. "Serafina is at——"

"It's the binding spell," Nyssa interrupts. "It's preventing her from giving away Serafina's location."

"I'm not under any spell," Arina spews.

"How long have you had the moon-shaped mole behind your ear?"

"It's a goddamn mole. I don't know…since being human?"

"She's lying," Alex announces. "It appeared a few days ago. She showed it to us earlier."

"Get out of my head, you little freak!"

"When we transition into becoming a vampire, all blemishes, moles, birthmarks, etc., disappear. That would mean the moon wasn't on you as a human," Fran interrupts. "You have been placed under her spell. You will do what she tells you to do."

"Fuck you, vamp."

"Tell us where she is." Brayden steps forward. He holds his hand up dramatically. "If I snap, you're returning. One, two, th…"

"Serafina is at——. Holy fuck!" she shouts.

"Nyssa, is there something we can do that will allow her to speak?" I ask the druid lycanthrope.

"Maybe." She locks eyes with Connor. "Can you get me a few things?"

"Sure?" the Alpha answers, not sounding convinced. "What do you need?"

"Water, some fresh soil, and salt."

"I'll be right back." Connor leaves the steel cell.

"Can I help?" Brayden asks.

"Normally, I would say no, but I might need your power."

"Good." He moves to her side just as Connor hurries back into the room, carrying the items Nyssa requested.

"Tell me what to do with them," he says, placing them on the concrete floor.

"Thank you, but there's nothing you can do."

"What the hell are you doing?" Arina asks. "Get away from me, witch."

"She's helping you," Autumn says. "And you need to learn some manners." I huff a laugh at the immortal child's words.

"Brayden, use the soil and make a circle around Arina." Brayden follows directions, spreading the cup of dirt around the angry vampire. "Now, cover the dirt with the salt and pour the water over her head."

Brayden moves close with the cup in his hands. "If you pour that on me, I'll kill you," Arina warns.

"If you touch one hair on his head, you won't have the opportunity to live a second longer." Fran steps forward. "Am I making myself clear?" I've never seen Fran in protective mode. She's terrifying and awe-inspiring at the same time.

Arina hisses in response. Something I've only witnessed a handful of vampires do before.

Nyssa turns toward the rest of us. "Everyone except Brayden and Elsie, out."

"If you for one minute think—" Fran starts.

"Out!" Nyssa shouts. "We're running out of time." She turns toward Connor. "Lock us inside."

"Nyssa?" I question. "Brayden?"

"I'll be fine," he reassures me.

Connor herds everyone through the door of the cell and into a protected area of the room. Nyssa waits for the lock to be secured before she takes mine and Brayden's hands into hers. "Lend me your power."

I close my eyes, reaching into my core and sending the strength that I used earlier straight into Nyssa. The sense of energy sliding through my body is a new and strange feeling.

"Chains unseen, release thy hold, for truth to burn where lies are cold. By root and claw, by storm and sea, speak now, by my decree." I open my eyes, seeing the air around us begin to shimmer with what can only be described as power. The air surrounding Arina begins to glow a light shade of green.

"What's that?" I whisper.

"The binding," Nyssa answers.

"Where is Serafina?" I ask for the last time.

"She's in the clouds," Arina answers. Her body recoils as her head falls backward. The scream that leaves her mouth is something primal. It's a mixture of pain and anger rolled into one. "It hurts!" she screams. "Make it go away!" Arina collapses to the floor of the cell.

"Is she dead?" Brayden asks.

"No. Her body is still here."

Several minutes pass with no one speaking. "She knows..." Arina whispers.

"Who knows?" I ask.

"Serafina!" Arina screams in pain again as her body lifts from the cement floor. The green aura that surrounded her moments earlier returns, darker in color as her body contorts. Her bound arms lift high above her head, cracking her bones in the process. Long legs pull forward, wrapping around her distorted body.

"Elsie," Fran warns from the other side of the cell.

"I know." Wrapping my arms around Brayden, I pull him toward the door at vampire speed. Behind us, Arina continues to scream, her body being broken beyond repair.

"What's happening to her?" Everly asks.

"Serafina knows we broke through," Nyssa answers. "My spell is wearing off, and the binding spell is returning."

"Elsie? We can't leave her like that," Alex says, moving to my side. "She's in pain."

"Kill me!" Arina screams from inside the cell.

"Holy shit," Connor exclaims. "What kind of magic is this?"

"Ancient," Nyssa answers. She turns toward me.

"Serafina will continue to torture her for eternity. Because she's a vampire, she'll never die. She'll be in eternal pain."

Moments of life with Kragen flash to mind. A life the two of us have in common. If I were in her situation, what would I want? I close my eyes, knowing the answer.

"I can help." Brayden steps in front of me.

"No." Glancing at Fran and Nyssa, I nod toward the door that leads back into the lycan bar. Both nod, understanding my intention.

Seconds later, Arina and I are the only people in the room. She continues to writhe in pain and scream as her body shifts into positions a body shouldn't. Stepping back into her cell, I move in front of the once beautiful woman.

"Do it," she whispers. "I'm begging you."

"I'm sorry, Arina."

"I'm not." She pants. "It's time." An ear-piercing scream follows her words as her torso is turned backward, nearly splitting her body in half. Bruises cover her skin, and several ribs are visible on the outside.

The only way to permanently kill a vampire is with a stake through the heart or decapitation and burning the body. I pull on the power of my ancestry, bringing the power to the surface.

"Do it!" A large knife slides across the floor behind me, landing at my feet. I turn, finding Cam standing on the other side of the bars. I don't know when he came back in the room, but I don't question it. He nods, and I slowly pick up the weapon.

"It's silver," he answers my unspoken question.

I lift the knife and, without thought, slice through Arina's tortured body, sending her head to the concrete below. "Burn," I whisper. In an instant, her head and body are engulfed in flames.

My legs collapse beneath me, lowering me to the concrete next to her. "I'm so sorry," I whisper.

"You didn't kill her. Serafina did." Cam moves to my side, wrapping an arm around my shoulders, and ushers me through the cell door. I've never been an overly emotional person, but at this moment, I need physical touch. I turn, wrapping my arms around his strong torso. He keeps his arms around my back until the tears stop falling.

"I've never felt like this after killing," I admit.

"Maybe it's because you shared the same maker."

I pull back, putting space between the two of us. "Thank you, Cam."

He smiles, reminding me of his older brother. "Think of me as an emotional support puppy." His words bring a well-needed smile to my face.

"Don't let them know I was weak."

"Elsie, you were anything but weak. What you just did was the most humane act I've witnessed from a vampire...ever. Truth be told, I don't know if I could've done the same."

I wipe the tear stains from my face and nod as he

opens the door. "It's done," I announce to the awaiting crowd. Nyssa, Connor, and Fran have a laptop in front of them while the children are sitting against the wall in silence. There's no doubt they heard everything that happened in the room.

"I'm sorry, Elsie," Alex's voice says through my mind.

"Me, too." Everly and Autumn add in unison.

"Thank you. I'm sorry you had to hear that."

"Elsie, we don't have a clue what Arina meant about Serafina's home being in the clouds," Fran announces.

"Google isn't going to have the answer. How the hell are we going to find somewhere that's hidden in the clouds? What does that even mean? A floating city?" I lower my head into my hands. "Thorne is there, being held by this woman. What if, when we find him, he ends up like Arina? What if..."

"He won't be," Fran answers, moving to my side. "Thorne is strong."

"What I witnessed in that room had nothing to do with strength. Arina was folded like a paper doll and would've been living the same nightmare over and over for an eternity. I can't let that happen to him."

"It won't," Alex answers. "We won't let it. We're going to find him."

"How?" I shout. "In the clouds?"

"Maybe it's fog," Everly answers.

"Or, an illusion." Brayden adds.

"What do we know about this witch, Serafina?" Connor asks.

"Other than she's insanely powerful and wants to steal my brother's spell—nothing."

"There's something familiar about what she said, about being in the clouds," he continues.

"What are you talking about?" Fran asks.

"I'll be right back." Connor excuses himself, leaving us alone in the backroom of the bar.

"This sucks," I announce to the room. I'm no stranger to the feeling of powerlessness. At this moment, the overwhelming sensation threatens to take over.

"I found it," Connor bursts back through the door, carrying a large book. I laugh at the irony. A book is what got us into this mess to start with. Meeting Phyllis in the library and finding Aaron's grimoire seems like a million years ago. The amount of shit that has gone down since then is nearly impossible to fathom.

Setting the book on a high-top bar table, he thumbs through the pages of an older bound text. He stops, pointing at a specific page. "Here it is. The vanishing manor."

"The vanishing manor?" I repeat, not sure I understood him correctly.

"Yeah. The story tells of an antebellum mansion hidden deep in the wetlands—a home so grand it rivaled the estates of Charleston's wealthiest families." He pulls the book closer to his face and reads, *"While some believe the house moves and is hidden by magic, the truth is the house has remained in its location for centuries if one knows where to look.*"

"That says a whole lot of nothing," Nyssa announces.

"*The home is called the House in the Clouds because, when the fog rolls in, the mansion seems to rise from the earth, floating like a vision from another world,*" Connor continues.

"Where is this house in the clouds?" Fran asks.

"No one knows." Connor closes the book dramatically.

"That was incredibly helpful, thank you." Fran sounds as frustrated as I feel. I resist the temptation to smirk at her sarcasm.

"Actually, it is," Nyssa says, moving to the center of the room. "Brayden?" She holds her hand toward the immortal child.

He latches onto her hand. "What are we doing?"

"I'm going to use the elements to look for any anomalies nearby. That might give us a clue where to look. Close your eyes, and open your mind. Lend me your power."

The two of them stand facing each other with their hands latched together. It doesn't take long before the room begins to *feel* different. Brayden's head flies back, and his eyes roll back in his head while Nyssa begins to shake slightly.

"What the hell?" Cam asks. "Do we need to do something?"

"I don't know," I answer truthfully.

Nyssa releases Brayden's hands, and he falls to the ground with a thud. I rush to his side, lifting him. "I'm okay." He pants. He's on his feet seconds later as Nyssa stops shaking and opens her eyes.

"We found it."

the plan..finally

"I NEED A MAP," Nyssa announces to everyone in the room. "Now!" Connor exits the room for the third time, returning seconds later with a folded map in his hands.

"This is old. A few landmarks may have changed since it was printed." He hands the rectangle-shaped paper to her.

Nyssa takes the map, spreading it open on the floor. She runs her finger across the cartography, moving toward the wetlands and marshy area of Charleston. "It's here," she says, pointing at a small inlet.

Connor pulls the map closer to his face. "Are you sure?"

"No," she answers. "While looking for Serafina's energy, we rode the wind. This is where reality was distorted."

"Explain," Cam interrupts. "Not the wind part, the distorted part."

"Everywhere else the wind took us felt normal, like it is here. When we went over that spot, the energy shifted, kind of like watching static on a television set."

Fran sets the computer down. "According to city records, that land is nothing but marsh and has been for centuries. It's uninhabitable."

"She's there," Brayden answers. "Nyssa is right. The energy was weird there. I felt it, too."

"What if we go and there's nothing there?" Fran asks.

"Then she's not there," I answer. "We don't have anything to lose."

"I'm afraid I can't go with you," Connor says, folding the map back to normal size. "I'm leaving in thirty minutes for New Orleans." He looks at Cam. "Your brother has called me down there to figure this out."

"We have enough," I answer for the group. Each person in our group has a gift, a reason for being here. Nothing against the alpha lycanthrope, but he will be deadweight in this situation.

"Okay. I'll leave you to it." Connor exits the room, leaving us alone.

"We need a plan, Elsie. There's none of this going in blindly thing that can happen here." Fran pauses, rubbing her temples. "I'm hesitant to say this, but we saw what happened to Arina when Nyssa pushed through Serafina's binding spell. What if that happens to Thorne?"

"I know."

"Let's go to my home here in Charleston. I have a replica there of my computer room in New Orleans. We can take a closer look at this marshland and come up with a strategic plan." Fran's eyes soften as she speaks. "You don't have to do this on your own. Let us help."

"You have a home here?" Out of everything she just said, I'm stuck on the fact that she owns a home in my city.

"It belonged to Viktor. Are you going to let us help?"

"Aye. I am letting you help."

Fran wraps her arm through mine. "No. You're the vampire on the run from her maker, trying to figure everything out on her own. You can trust us. We're here for you, and you don't have to do it alone."

I open my mouth to argue and realize she's right. Other than depending on a few spells from Phyllis and Nyssa, I'm doing what I always do. I'm taking the burden onto myself. It's what I've always done. "Okay," I whisper.

No one speaks on the drive back to Fran's house. Cam pulls Phyllis's SUV to a stop behind the three-story home not far from the rental Thorne, and I have been in.

The eight of us pile through the back door into a dimly lit kitchen. "There's goat's blood in the fridge and some fresh lunch meat and bread for those that eat food."

"Oh, thank God. I'm starved," Cam announces, heading straight for the food. The children follow him, pulling several bottles of red liquid from the door.

"Elsie, you should eat," Cam says, handing me a bottle of blood. My stomach growls at the sight.

"Thirty minutes," I announce, slamming the empty bottle on the counter. "I need a shower."

"Thirty minutes," Fran agrees. "I'll get everything up and running."

I head up the back stairway to the second floor and to one of the only rooms with the door standing open. Like the rest of the home, the room is immaculately decorated. A beautiful four-poster bed, perfectly in tune with the age of the home, sits against the far wall. The mahogany posts are intricately carved, with ornate images of grain and rice. The bedding is soft and delicate, the perfect opposition of the masculine wooden frame. A large fireplace covers one wall, and the ceiling is painted haint blue—something used often in old Southern homes.

The wardrobe holds a few clothes that probably belong to Amelia or Celeste. I'm going to hope they fit. I grab what looks like workout attire before heading into the en suite bathroom, thankfully fully stocked with all the necessities. I take a longer-than-needed shower, letting the water take away a little of the tension I've been holding onto since Thorne left with Serafina. Hell, who am I kidding? I've held tension for over three hundred years.

Ten minutes later, I'm sitting in Fran's computer room, surrounded by the people who have sworn to help me. Alex moves to my side as I enter, offering warm energy through our connection. Everly, Autumn, and Brayden look through Fran's laptop computer collection, studying each piece carefully.

"You look better," Fran says with a grin.

"I feel a bit better, thank you."

Fran pulls up a map on a large screen in front of us. "What's that?" Alex asks.

"This is an aerial view of the marsh Nyssa identified earlier. It's a satellite image from a few years back."

"There's nothing there," Everly states the obvious.

"Nyssa? Do you see anything?" I ask.

"Through human eyes, no." She steps closer to the screen. "However, the energy is *off*."

"I see it," Brayden adds. "The air is shimmery."

"I'm going to have to take your word on that, buddy," Cam says, ruffling the immortal child's hair.

Everly steps close to Brayden. "I see it, too."

Staring at the image on the screen, I force myself to see what they see. Nothing appears. "I don't see anything but marshland and haze."

"You're seeing the illusion. You have to look through it to see what's really there," Brayden says.

"It's like one of the old 3D images that you stare at long enough that the image changes into something completely different. Clear your mind of any expectations of what should be there, and allow your eyes to focus on what's really there." Nyssa moves closer to the image as she speaks, pointing at a dark spot on the screen. "Keep looking here."

I follow instructions, wiping my mind clear and staring at the spot she pointed out. I'm not sure if it's a figment of my imagination, but for a brief moment, the image of a roof comes into view. I blink several times, trying to clear my eyes. "I...I think I saw something."

"What did you see?" Alex asks.

"The outline of something. A roof, maybe? I'm not sure."

Cam moves in front of the large screen. "Where again?" Nyssa points to the same spot on the screen, and Cam stares for several minutes. "Yeah, I don't see anything."

"Fran? Do you have any other images of the area?" I ask.

"This came from Google Earth. Give me a minute. I can hack into a few government sites and find more current images." I don't question the computer genius vampire as she types away at the main keyboard of her setup. To the untrained eye, mine, it looks like she's typing a series of numbers onto a black screen.

"Got it," she announces. "This image is from two days ago." A new picture pulls up on the large screen. The grass is greener than in the first image. Other than that, nothing has changed.

"It looks the same," Autumn announces.

"No, it doesn't." Nyssa moves closer. "There's something here. I feel the energy of the illusion and something else."

"What?" Cam asks.

"Serafina." Brayden fills in the blank. "I feel her."

I fight the tears threatening to fall. "That means Thorne is there."

"What if he's not?" Alex asks, wrapping his arm through mine.

"Then we kill Serafina anyway."

Fran turns in the computer chair she's occupying. "Elsie, don't lose your brains now. The whole reason we came back here was to form a plan. We can't do this half-ass." She looks around the room. "Every person in this room is an instrumental part of the plan. Each person has special abilities and gifts that will be needed. Without a plan, we won't survive. Any of us."

"She's just a witch," I remind her.

"She's a witch with a powerful bloodline," Nyssa reminds me. "She will stop at nothing to get into that grimoire."

"Maybe she's saving the siphon spell until we're there," Alex adds.

"Why would she do that?"

"To watch us suffer," Brayden answers with a shrug.

I glance at the ancient clock hanging on the wall. "It's five o'clock. I refuse to leave Thorne there, under her binding, longer than necessary. Yes, we need a plan, but we need it now. I'm done waiting around."

Our group gathers together, forming a circle in the middle of the room. "Other than finding the possible location of the house, what other major conflicts are we up against?" Cam takes a leadership role, and I'm grateful.

"Serafina will use her illusions to confuse us. Turn us against one another, lead us into traps, etc.," Nyssa answers.

"The bound will come to her defense," Fran adds. "They will fight to the death to protect her."

"Arina didn't." Brayden crosses his arms over his chest. "She relented to the illusion of her captivity."

"Aye, but not all vampires have a story like the one Arina and I share. We don't have the resources or time to discover each one's background for illusion creation. We have to assume they're willing to die for her."

"What about the bound lycan?" Cam asks.

"Unless we're able to produce a spell that will unbind them, they'll be bound until Serafina's death." Nyssa leans back in her chair.

"So, basically, it's kill or be killed." Cam's tone is flat.

"I can communicate with everyone while we're there. If anyone has a question about something being real or an illusion, I can connect us together and to Brayden and Nyssa." Alex smiles as he speaks.

"I will create illusions of my own to confuse Serafina and the bound." Brayden piggybacks onto Alex's idea.

Nyssa props her hands on her hips. "I can cast a spell that will enchant our group and enable us to move undetected by any magical wards while Brayden camouflages our group's arrival from any lookouts or guards."

"I could distract them by moving objects around in front of them," Autumn adds.

"Unless you can move a tree on command, I'm not sure that will be helpful," Fran answers.

Autumn's tiny shoulders shrug. "That's not a problem."

"I can mimic everyone's powers and go where help is needed," Everly adds.

Fran turns toward me. "That leaves you, me, and Cam to find Thorne, get the grimoire, and fix this entire shit show."

I shake my head. "We're going to need to work together. She's going to try to separate us and turn us against one another. We can't let that happen." I look at each member of the group. "Your ideas are great, except for one thing. We have to stay together at all times. I will not sacrifice any of you. The moment we're separated, her illusions will take effect. She could take the form of any of us at any time. The only way to protect everyone is to stay together."

"No one is planning on sacrificing anything," Cam answers for the group. "We each have a role to play, and we're ready to play it. None of us is dumb enough to think everything will work out the way we plan, but knowing what our goal is and each person's role in that goal is the way to defeat her."

"Aye, but we stay together. That's not up for discussion." I look around the room, making eye contact with each member of our team. Each nod, understanding my insistence. "We have to make sure Serafina dies," I add. "If she lives, the binding spell will live with her. Nyssa's unbinding spell will only lead to more situations like Arina's."

"This isn't a plan," Fran says grimly.

"I think I can speak for everyone here when I say there's no way to form a plan to attack when we don't know what we're walking into. Each person has a skill, and we have a plan on how to utilize that skill. What's going to happen when we get there? We have no way of knowing." Nyssa moves toward the large monitor. "This is our plan." She points at the void once more. "This is where she is. This is where Thorne and who knows how many more are. This is where the grimoire is." She pauses. "This is our plan."

"What are we waiting on?" I ask.

"Nothing," Cam answers. "I'll get the SUV."

"This plan sucks," Fran mumbles, ushering the children toward the door and making me smile. She's right.

sibling rivalry

THE TRIP toward the wetlands is relatively quiet as Cam follows Nyssa's directions through the empty terrain. The further we go, the stronger the energy becomes. I don't see any physical changes in the environment, but I feel them. I don't know if that's the vampire in me or the witch.

"How close should we get?" Fran asks from the back seat.

"I think this is close enough," Nyssa answers. "Cam, can you hide the car in there?" She points toward a grouping of overgrown bushes.

"Yeah, but it's going to do a hell of a job on the paint." The rest of us climb out before Cam speeds into the greenery. By the time he stops, only a small portion of the roof is visible. A few minutes later, he walks around the bushes with a few new scratches and his hair disheveled. "That should keep it hidden," he says, running his fingers through his mop-top.

"We walk from here." Nyssa takes over.

"How far is it?" Fran asks.

Nyssa sighs before answering. "Mileage-wise, I don't know. Energy-wise, it is not far. There are protections in place not far from here." She turns toward Brayden. "Can you camouflage us?"

The immortal child closes his eyes, takes a deep breath in, and slowly lets it out. "Done," he says with a smile. "I made us look and feel like a flock of ducks."

"That's pretty smart, Brayden." I pat his back with my words. "Remember, we have to stick together. No matter what, we cannot separate from each other."

"We know," the group says in unison.

"Elsie?" Nyssa calls from the front of our group. I move quickly to her side. "You need to know I performed a spell before we left."

"What kind of spell?" I'm not sure whether I should be concerned or relieved.

"A tracking spell." Her words are softer. "Specifically for Thorne."

I stop walking. "And?"

She hands me a soft pink crystal with a faint glow. "The spell connected this stone to Thorne's energy. The closer he is, the brighter the stone will glow."

"It's glowing now."

"That's why I'm giving it to you." She smiles. "It

wasn't glowing until a few minutes ago. We're going the right way, and he's there."

Clutching my fingers around the stone, I pull it to my heart. For now, it's the only lifeline I have to Thorne.

The further we move, the stronger the energy becomes. I open my fingers to find the stone glowing brighter than before. "We're close," I whisper to Nyssa.

"It's just around this bend," she answers. "Squeeze closer together." She motions toward the small group behind us. They follow orders, and in an instant, we're huddled together.

"Testing, testing," Alex says through my mind. *"If you can hear me, nod your head."* To my surprise, everyone in our group nods.

"Can you hear me?" Everly echoes, mimicking Alex's ability. Again, everyone nods.

"Can we hear each other?" I ask. Other than the immortal children, no one responds. "Well, that answers that question," I say aloud.

"When we get there, Brayden, keep up the duck illusion. No matter what you hear or think you hear, keep the illusion in place. Do you understand me?" Nyssa orders. "Once she discovers we're here, she's going to throw every trick in her book at us." Brayden nods. We start moving again, and the crystal glows even brighter. I focus on staying in the moment and not letting the excitement of finding Thorne overtake the mission.

"Nyssa says it's just around the corner," Alex translates. *"She says to be ready for anything."*

Following the landscape, we circle around a heavy bend, surrounded by a thick marsh on either side. Nyssa stops walking as we reach what looks like a dead end. The crystal glows brighter as I stare into the empty space in front of us. I feel something, but see nothing.

"This is it." Alex wraps his fingers through mine, no doubt feeling my uneasiness. Brayden moves closer to Nyssa, and the two of them hold hands. *"Nyssa and Brayden are doing a spell to make the house visible."*

Seconds later, the illusion shatters like glass, and the shimmering haze melts away to reveal the truth beneath. It's almost as if the air is holding its breath before the antebellum home emerges in full view, standing like a ghost on the marshland. The stately home is weathered but regal, with towering white columns reaching up to a sagging roof draped in creeping ivy.

Once white paint has faded to a cracked and peeling haunting gray color. Arched windows seem to watch as we move closer, their glass glowing with an eerie light. Moss and vines crawl up the sides, wrapping the house in its protection, while the high steps leading to the front door appear as if time had forgotten what they're used for.

The marshland around us buzzes with an unnatural stillness—no wind, no bird calls, only the soft lapping of water against the muddy banks. Yet the air feels heavy, almost as if the house itself pulses with life, daring anyone to enter.

"That's terrifying," Alex whispers through my mind.

"Aye, it is."

His fingers grip mine slightly tighter as he stares at the door of the home, watching it creak open and two lycan step out. Dressed in their usual uniform of worn jeans and button-down shirts, they look every bit the part of stoic guards.

The door swings open again, and this time, a woman emerges—her presence striking, as though she'd walked off the pages of a fashion magazine. The energy rolling off her is unmistakably vampire. It pulses toward me like a warning. She halts mid-step. Her head lifts as she sniffs the air around her. Shit. Does she sense us?

Nyssa turns toward Brayden, who nods at a silent question passed between them. She moves closer to the house, dangerously close to the lycan who are walking the perimeter. Our group follows close behind.

"Do you feel something strange?" the vampire asks the two men.

"Nothing but you, bloodsucker."

The woman scoffs, moving away from the lycan. *"She senses us."* I move protectively in front of Alex, who's still holding onto my hand.

"We're still an illusion," Brayden answers telepathically. *"She may sense us, but she doesn't understand what she's feeling."*

"Let's hope you're right."

The two lycan pass us, completely unaware. Slowly, our group moves toward the oversized front entrance, stopping at the bottom of the stairs. The front door opens, and my heart leaps into my throat. Framed in the doorway is the man I've loved for three centuries—Captain Hawthorne Rex.

"Don't react," Alex warns. *"He can't see us."*

"He's stronger than you think," I remind him.

"She's right," Thorne's deep voice resonates through my mind. *"I am stronger than you think, and I see you...all of you."* He looks around our small group, making eye contact with each member. *"Why are you here?"*

"To save you," Everly's soft voice answers.

"I don't need saving."

"Serafina bound you to her," I answer. *"You're not yourself."*

"That's where you're wrong, Elsbeth. I've never been more myself."

"Her spell has a hold on you." I turn toward Brayden. *"Let me out of the illusion."*

"Elsie, no! You'll be visible to everyone, not just Thorne," he argues.

"I know." I pause, staring into the large eyes of the immortal child. *"It's okay,"* I whisper. Energy sweeps over me, and the illusion leaves.

"I could see you before," Thorne's deep voice echoes. *"The theatrics weren't necessary."*

"I'm here," I answer, stepping closer. *"You're not

yourself. The Thorne I know would never have left of his own free will."

"Maybe you don't know me as well as you thought you did," he retorts.

"The Thorne I know is strong, brilliant, and willing to sacrifice his life for others. You stalked a vampire and convinced him to turn you into the very thing you despised just to find me. You did that selflessly."

Thorne laughs. "There was nothing selfless about that. I left my wife and son to become a monster."

The female vampire from before moves to Thorne's side. "I knew I smelled something." She turns, rubbing her hands along his chest. "Want me to kill her?"

"No," he answers quickly. "Leave us."

The woman steps back. "I don't remember you being in charge."

Thorne turns. "I am now. Leave, or I'll make you leave."

The woman glances between the two of us before sniffing the air. "She's not alone." She turns, moving back inside the ancient home.

"Thorne, you need to come with us," I continue.

"I don't *need* to do anything. I'm here because this is where I want to be. Serafina is my future."

"Your future? Are you...Are you sleeping with her?"

He scrunches his face. "No, she's my sister."

"Don't you see? She has her magic woven so intricately around you that you believe you're here of your own free will."

"Dammit, Elsie. I *am* here of my own free will. Not everything revolves around you! I know that concept may be difficult for you to perceive, but wake the hell up." His words hurt more than I let on, and I fight the tears threatening to fall.

The energy shifts, and Brayden moves to my side. "What did you do?"

The immortal child ignores my question, turning toward Thorne. "Serafina is manipulating you."

"Nothing personal, kid, but you were human a few months ago. How old are you? Seven...eight?"

"My age doesn't matter. We share the same gifts, you and I."

"And me." The energy shifts once more, and Nyssa moves next to Brayden. "We share a common bond through our blood."

"My father got around, didn't he?"

Nyssa ignores his jab. "You hold druid blood in you, a small amount, but enough to give you power. It was passed down through your mother's side. It explains your abilities..." Nyssa grunts loudly, stopping her words mid-sentence. She stands firm and glares at Thorne while holding her side in pain.

"Is this the ability you're speaking of?"

"You're not stronger than me," she retorts.

"I have your blood in me. Did you forget your little ritual?" He raises his hand toward Nyssa.

"Stop!" I shout. "Thorne, this isn't you. Brayden's

right. Serafina is manipulating you to think this is the real you. It's not."

"You knew me for a month, Elsie. One month of me being your captain. I took pity on a starving young girl and fed her. It was nothing more than pity and lust."

"Thorne, you don't mean that."

"See, that's the thing. I do." He crosses his arms over his chest. "I was nothing more than a horny young man looking for his next conquest." Thorne's words cut deep. Out of the two of us, I'm the one with hurtful words. Thorne is calm, levelheaded, and kind.

"Now, Brayden," Nyssa whispers toward the immortal child.

"By root and stone, by blood and breath, awake the truth that sleeps in death. Let shadows break, let falsehoods flee, druid heart, now rise to see!" Brayden steps backward a few steps after his words.

"What the hell was that?" I ask, not sure what just happened. Turning toward Thorne, I see it. His face has gone from angry and firm to the Thorne I'm used to seeing. Softness has returned to his features. "Thorne?" I whisper.

He blinks a few times, seemingly clearing the haze from his eyes. Hardness returns to his face as he looks at the druids in front of him. "What did you do to me?"

"It was a spell to awaken your druid blood. What we did before wasn't as strong," Nyssa answers, stepping in front of Brayden.

"It worked," Alex says, moving to my side. "Look at him."

"Nothing worked. I was kind enough to let you and this ragtag group of misfits stay on this land. That time is over. If you're not gone in ten seconds, I will kill you." He looks me in the eyes. "*All* of you."

"No," I retort. "We're not leaving until Serafina is dead and you're home." I just revealed the entirety of our plan in one sentence.

Thorne's laugh echoes off the water. "You don't stand a chance against her."

Leaving the presumed safety of our group, I move up the ancient steps until I'm inches away from Thorne. "You're in there. The man I fell in love with at nineteen years old—he's in there. I feel him."

"Go..." he starts.

"Do you remember the night he took me?" I ask, interrupting his dismissal. "The night Kragen boarded your ship, killing Charles before taking me?" Thorne's expression remains stoic. I look him in the eyes. "You were willing to sacrifice yourself to save me, but I wouldn't allow it. I chose to go with him to save you and everyone aboard that ship, including my family. That Thorne is still in there. The man who was willing to lay down his life to save the starving farm girl." The last part is no louder than a whisper.

Thorne's pupils dilate as he looks at me. "Elsie?"

I place my hand on his cheek. "Aye, my love. It's me."

The front door opens, revealing the woman we're here to kill. Serafina stands in the doorframe, wearing a long black dress and an iconic witch's hat. "Well, look who the cat dragged in." She snaps her fingers. "Hawthorne." At the sound of his name, his pupils return to their normal size, and he moves to his binder's side. "Kill them, dear brother."

the power of a child

"THORNE?" I question, hoping to break through the barrier once more. "We're here to help you."

"He doesn't need your help," Serafina spews. She looks around our group. "You brought children to fight for you?" Her laugh echoes off the still water. "And I'm the one with the bad reputation."

"We're not children," Alex answers.

"Dear boy, from my viewpoint, you're children." Serafina's movements remind me of a lycan, as she sniffs the air in front of her. "You all have the same maker, except for you." She points at Brayden. "You're different." She sniffs the air once more. "Very different."

Nyssa moves protectively in front of the immortal child. "Leave them alone."

Serafina laughs again. "I'm not the one who brought children to a rescue party. That is what we're calling it, right?" She claps her hands loudly. "You're here to rescue poor, helpless Hawthorne, who's being held against his will…blah, blah, blah."

"Let him go," I warn.

"Or what?" Serafina stalks closer. "You're nothing more than…" She pauses. "What were the words you used again? A starving farm girl? Yes, that's it." Her words bring anger to the surface.

"I'm more than you know." My words sound like a middle school kid standing up to their bully.

"That little twinge of witch blood you carry around doesn't mean much in the big scheme of things," she taunts.

"You need me."

Her laugh is louder than before, carried in the fog that surrounds us. "I don't need anyone."

"You need me to open Aaron's grimoire." The smile that covered her face earlier is gone. "You did all of this to get your hands on his spell. But, oops, you can't open the grimoire, can you?"

"I don't need Aaron's spells."

"Then why steal the grimoire?" Cam asks.

"What do you know, wolf?" she spews.

"I know that you want Aaron's spell," he retorts, making me smile.

"Would you like us to kill them?" a deep voice says from behind. Turning, I find the lycan who were walking the perimeter earlier looming over our group.

"Back off, or I will make you back off," Cam warns.

"Fuck you, St. James," one of the men answers as the two of them shift into larger-than-life wolves.

Cam doesn't waste a minute, transforming into an even larger version. *"I'll take care of these two assholes. Nyssa, stay with Elsie and the children."* His words ring through my mind just as he jumps toward the two wolves.

"Brayden, can you confuse the two lycan and vampire?" I ask.

"I...I don't know what to do." His voice sounds more anxious than usual.

"Make them think they're in the cage at the bar."

Cam steps back as the two lycan stop fighting and move closer to each other. Both look around, confusion filling their expression. The larger of the two jumps against the invisible walls, unable to breach their hold.

"Holy shit," Cam says through my mind. *"I can't believe that worked."*

Serafina claps slowly from the doorframe. "That was impressive." Her voice is void of emotion. She turns toward Brayden. "Druid. That's what I smell on you. Imagine that. Two druids in one place."

"Three," Nyssa says, stepping even closer.

"Would you look at that? Not so extinct, are you, dear brother?"

"You're the only one strong enough to defeat her. That's why she bound you to her," I interrupt the moment of insanity.

"Hawthorne, don't listen to her. You're my brother—my family. The last remaining tie to our heritage."

"Are they bound?" Thorne looks at the two lycan and vampire, seemingly trapped in a silver cage. "Am I bound?"

"She wants Aaron's spell," I answer quickly. "A spell to siphon death."

"I don't know what that means," he answers, looking between the two of us.

"She will take the one thing that's kept us alive. Our affliction. We will no longer be vampires."

Thorne turns fully toward his sister. "Is this true?"

"Enough!" Serafina yells. Long arms raise high above her head as she begins to chant in an ancient language. With her words, Thorne's face becomes stoic, almost robotic.

"It's a binding spell," Brayden says through my mind. *"It's stronger than the first. He can't fight her."*

"Kill them," Serafina whispers. "Kill them now."

A horde of vampires and lycan comes from nowhere, surrounding our small group. "No!" I shout. "This doesn't have to end like this."

"Open the grimoire, Elsbeth, and I'll stop it before it begins." Serafina's words strike deep.

"No!" Fran speaks for the first time. "If you open that grimoire, more than us will die. I don't know about you, but I'd rather die fighting."

"Aye," I answer, turning toward the love of my life. The smile that covers his face is a mixture of cruelty and evil. "Protect the children," I charge the adults beside me. "I'll take care of Thorne."

"What about Serafina?" Brayden asks.

"She's ours," Nyssa answers, wrapping her fingers through the immortal child's. "We're stronger together. Thorne's not the only one powerful enough to defeat her."

Without warning, Thorne bares his teeth and jumps on me, knocking me several yards back. What the hell? "Thorne! This isn't you."

"It's me, Elsbeth." He rushes me, knocking me in the stomach and back the length of a football field to the edge of the water. "It's always been me."

I stand, wiping the mud off my pants. "You're kind and gentle. This has never been you. You fed a helpless, starving girl when she..."

"Oh, stop it, Elsie. I'm tired of hearing that boring story. You've never been helpless. Starving, maybe. But helpless? Never." He's in front of me seconds later.

"I love you, Thorne. I've always loved you." For a brief moment, Thorne's eyes dilate, like before. "I love you," I repeat.

"*Elsie, now!*" Brayden shouts through my mind. Tears fill my eyes as I allow the power to grow inside. The sensation fills my core, working its way upward.

"Thorne, I don't want to do this."

"Elsie?" Thorne says, his voice regaining its normal timbre. "What..." He stops mid-sentence, holding either side of his head as he screams in agony. Standing on the front porch is Serafina. Her hands are wide to her side as she chants in the same language as before.

"Elsie! Do it," Brayden repeats his words.

"I'm sorry," I whisper, fighting through the tears as I send the power of my witch heritage into Thorne. Normally, I wouldn't be strong enough to overpower him with his Druid abilities, but with him torn between worlds, I have no doubt it will work. "Burn," I whisper, sending my power into the man I love, into the man who became a vampire to find me so many centuries ago. His body ignites instantly, and I collapse to the ground.

"Get up!" Fran demands, moving to my side. "Thorne's a vampire. Your fire will burn him, but not kill him. All you've done is disable him for a bit." She wraps her arms around mine, pulling me to my feet. "We need you right now, Elsie. The children need you. Get your shit together."

Thorne's body has collapsed to the ground, fully engulfed in flames. Fran's right. The flames won't kill him, but they'll keep him down for a while. I turn my attention toward the fight to see Alex, Autumn, and Everly working together as a unified, deadly killing machine. Three vampires lay in their wake, their heads separated from their bodies.

"You good?" she asks before disappearing in the blink of an eye to help the trio of destruction.

Cam is singlehandedly fighting an entire pack of wolves, holding his own against the mass of fur.

I turn my attention back to the house and the reason why we're here. Serafina's holding Aaron's grimoire in her hands, facing it toward the raging fight in front of her. Brayden and Nyssa are at the bottom of the stairs, being held in place by whatever Serafina is chanting. Without thinking, I move to their side, wrapping my fingers through Brayden's.

"Give me the grimoire," I warn.

Serafina stops chanting, turning her attention to the bottom of the stairs. "You are in no position to demand anything."

"Give me the grimoire," I repeat.

She laughs, making my skin crawl. "Unlock it, or I will kill him."

"You can't kill me," Brayden answers.

"Not you, dear one." She nods toward the burning body of Thorne. "Him."

"He's your brother," I retort.

"If you think that matters to me, you're dumber than I thought. He's just a means to an end. I knew you'd come to *save*," she mocks my voice, "the *love of your life*."

"You did all this just to get me to open the grimoire?"

Serafina shrugs. "Impressive, isn't it?"

"Innocent people have died," I retort.

"Innocent? Each one of the *bound* creatures drank from a human or ate fresh meat from a freshly slain animal. They're hardly innocent."

"Why?" Nyssa asks. "Why do you want Aaron's spell?"

The witch pulls the book to her chest. "Normally, I wouldn't honor you with my reasons, but since you're about to die, I'll indulge you." She looks away at a memory. "His name was Nathaniel, and he was, as you say, the love of my life." She pauses.

"I thought Aaron was your lover," I admit.

She laughs loudly. "Your brother was, how do I say this...he was not a fan of women. We were nothing more than friends until he..."

"Until he took the binding spell," Nyssa interrupts.

"No." Serafina looks up. "Until he made a bargain he couldn't keep. All because of you." Her eyes turn toward me. "He made a deal with your pirate."

"Kragen?"

"Aye. He made a deal with him. A spell in exchange for you."

"The siphoning spell," Brayden finishes.

"Good job, little druid. Yes, the siphoning spell. Imagine what a creature like him could've done with a spell like that."

"Kragen wasn't a witch. What could he have done with the spell?" I ask.

"The pirate was like you," Serafina answers. "It was in his bloodline. That's why he collected you. It's what he did. He collected *special* things."

"Holy shit." I knew that he took me because of my abilities, but had no idea we shared witch ancestry.

"Yes, holy shit, indeed, but you already knew that, didn't you?" I refuse to answer. "Aaron knew the power the spell would give Kragen and changed his mind. Your pirate didn't like that."

"He wasn't *my* pirate."

Serafina ignores my words. "When Aaron wouldn't give him the spell, he took revenge on the coven, including my Nathaniel. I watched as he drained him dry, leaving his body like it was nothing, like *he* was nothing." Her voice cracks as the memory fills her mind. "And for what? Power? To keep feeding on humans like parasites? You're all the same. You use, you take, you destroy—never stopping to see the carnage you leave behind."

"Kragen's dead," I remind her. "The siphoning spell won't do you any good against him."

"Your naivety is amusing." She laughs, holding the grimoire in front of her. "The siphoning spell will change that. It will take every bit of it and leave you as empty as the lives you've stolen. You think I'm cruel? You think I'm a monster? Maybe I am. But you brought this on yourselves. If I have to burn the world to stop your kind, so be it." She turns her eyes toward Brayden. "Look what you did to him. He's nothing more than a child. Now, he's a monster."

"Who's the monster here, Serafina? Look around you. This is all your doing. Killing every vampire won't bring Nathaniel back."

"It's a start." She raises her hands high in the air

with the grimoire held tightly in her hands. Serafina's voice drops to a chilling whisper. "There is no justice for Nathaniel. But I'll make sure the rest of you die for what you've done."

Brayden pulls his hand out of my grip and claps loudly. With the sound, the air begins to shimmer like heat rising from the scorched earth before fracturing, splitting reality apart with a soundless crack. One moment, Serafina's fury is palpable; the next, everything shifts. Shadows stretch unnaturally, swallowing the light, and the world dissolves into an endless expanse of black and gray.

The immortal child stands in the center of it all, his eyes glowing as his illusion holds firm. "You're in my world now," he says, his voice bouncing from every direction. "Here, we're equal."

the beginning of the end

"WHAT IS THIS?" Serafina asks, looking at the void that surrounds us.

"It's nothing," Brayden answers.

"Nonsense, it's just an illusion. A very good one, but nothing more." She moves, still clinging to Aaron's grimoire. "Quite impressive."

"Thank you," the immortal child answers, showing the innocence of his youth.

Serafina raises her hand and snaps. I don't know what she expected to happen, but remaining in the void with the three of us must not have been it. The surprised look on her face is almost comedic.

"I told you. Here, we're all equal." Brayden smiles.

The witch raises her hand, snapping once more, and again, nothing happens. "That's not possible."

"Apparently, it is," Nyssa answers. She raises her

hand, sending a blast into Serafina, knocking her back a few feet.

"You're no more powerful than the one who created the illusion," Brayden answers her unasked question. "A child."

Serafina clinches the grimoire under one arm, lifting the book high in the air. She begins to chant in an ancient language. I know without asking, she's casting a spell to escape Brayden's creation.

"It won't work," Nyssa interrupts. "Did you not hear the boy? In here, we're all equal."

"That's not possible," she retorts before attempting to cast the spell once more. Again, nothing happens.

"Give me the grimoire," I demand, stepping closer.

Serafina's dark eyes close as she clutches the book to her chest. "This is not how this is going to go." Her body begins to glow with an otherworldly light. She opens her eyes and smiles. "Go to hell." The glow rushes toward the three of us, resembling an explosive shock wave. The wave hits before any of us have time to react, throwing us in different directions. My body lands hard against a solid surface, slamming my head in the process. If that was Serafina with less power... damn.

A few seconds pass before I am able to stand. As a vampire, I'm immortal, but whatever she packed in that punch was stronger than me. I look around, finding nothing and no one. "Brayden? Nyssa?" Neither answer.

"Brayden?" I call through my mind. *"Nyssa?"* Neither answer. Fuck. I don't know where I am, let alone what to do.

"Trust in yourself," a voice says from all around me. The Scottish brogue takes me back three centuries to my life on the farm.

"Hello?"

"I'm here," the voice says directly behind me. I turn, finding the nearly exact image of my father, only different. "Papa?"

The man smiles a familiar smile. "No, Elsbeth. It's me, Aaron."

"How?" My words are no louder than a whisper.

"I am with you, always. Find me in the wind, in the flame, in the whispers of the moon. You are not lost. You were never lost to me," he quotes the letter I found in the grimoire at the start of this shit show.

"Are you really here?" I reach out, longing to touch the face of the man I last knew as an infant.

"Aye." He meets my hand halfway, pulling it to his face. He feels as solid as anything I've felt before.

"Is this an illusion?"

"Yes, and no. I am no longer on this earth. With that in mind, yes, I am an illusion." He looks around the darkness. "But here, I am whole."

"You look just like Papa."

"So, I've been told," he answers. "You look like Mama." He pauses. "She never gave up hope, you know."

"I'm so sorry, Aaron. I can't imagine what it must have been like."

"You owe no one an apology. You sacrificed your life to save us. It's the reason I created the spell."

"The siphoning spell?"

"Aye. I tried to trade the spell in return for your life." His eyes turn sad as he speaks.

"I know," I answer, hoping to ease his pain at the memory.

"In the end, I couldn't do it. I'm sorry, Elsbeth."

"Elsie," I interrupt. "Call me Elsie."

"By not giving Kragen the spell, I sacrificed your life once more."

"Kragen would've never let me go—spell or no spell." I wrap my hand around his. "Serafina has your grimoire."

"Serafina? How? She should be long since dead."

I laugh, echoing off the void. "She's alive and well and wants the siphoning spell."

"What would she want with that?"

"She wants to kill all of the vampires and a few lycan in retaliation for Nathaniel's death."

Aaron closes his eyes and walks a few steps backward. "That psycho bitch."

"That's an understatement."

"How did you get here?" he asks.

"It's a long story, but in short form, an illusion from a druid vampire."

He stares at me blankly with eyes I'd recognize

anywhere. "Did I understand you correctly? A druid vampire?"

"Aye." I smile. "He's only a child."

"An immortal child? Is he here, in the void, with you?"

"Aye. He and another druid. She's lycan."

The smile that covers Aaron's face is priceless. "You brought a druid vampire and a druid lycanthrope to the fight?"

"I like to come prepared." I smile back.

He turns, facing into the darkness. "They're this way. Let's go find them, shall we?" He reaches his hand toward me, grabbing hold of mine. In the blink of an eye, we're standing in front of Serafina with Nyssa and Brayden.

"Aaron Abernathy," Serafina says breathlessly. "How?"

"I could ask the same of you, Sera."

"Aaron? As in Elsie's brother, Aaron?" Nyssa asks.

"Aye." He turns his attention to the ancient witch. "Give Elsie my grimoire. The spell was not meant for you."

"Shut up," she spews. "This is another illusion by the boy."

Aaron turns toward the immortal child. "You're the druid vampire?"

"Yes." He shrugs.

Aaron turns toward Nyssa, "Druid lycanthrope?"

She nods.

"It's a pleasure to meet you both."

"Illusion or not, you do not own the grimoire. Give it to its rightful owner, now." Serafina raises her hands, the grimoire held tightly in her hands, and begins to chant. "Knock that shite off, Sera." A blast of energy hits the witch in the chest, causing her to bend slightly.

Serafina moves so quickly, even with vampire eyes, that I have trouble tracking her energy. A heartbeat later, she's standing in front of us with Brayden clinched in her arms. "Release me from this place," she warns.

"No," Brayden answers bravely.

"I will kill you," she continues. "Is that what you want, child?"

"If you kill me, you will stay here forever."

Without words, Aaron grips my hand tighter while wrapping his fingers around Nyssa's hand. I know without asking, he's requesting to borrow our power. I send every ounce I can muster through our joined hands. "Bound by blood, by will, by fire, return to me, as I require. Through shadowed path and ether's thread, come home, my own, where you are led."

With his words, the grimoire bursts into flames. Serafina's scream is a mixture of surprise and pain as the grimoire falls heavily to the floor. She's in the air with Brayden held tightly to her chest, seconds later. "Open the book, or the boy dies." She pulls a wooden stake out of thin air, pointing it at his tiny heart.

"No!" I scream. *"Brayden, do something!"*

"I can't," he answers. *"I don't have any energy left."*

"Let this illusion go. Save yourself."

"If I do, she'll kill everyone."

The sensation starts in my core, without thinking of what I'm doing, releasing my infant brother's hand, I lift off the ground until I'm even with the witch. "If you send that blast you're brewing into me, you'll kill the boy, too."

Seeing Brayden in Serafina's arms and his willingness to sacrifice himself to save everyone else brings my life full circle. *"You don't have to sacrifice yourself. We can fight her."*

"You did," his soft voice answers as I lower back to the ground.

"No," I whisper as Nyssa grabs hold of my arm.

"He's right," she answers. "If she gets out of here, she'll kill Alex, Autumn, Everly, Fran…"

"I get it," I interrupt. "Dammit, I get it!"

"It's okay, Elsie. I'll be okay."

"Brayden, don't ask me to do this."

"He's not," Nyssa answers, linking her arm through mine. "We don't have a choice." Without asking, Nyssa somehow grabs my power, pulling it from my body and combining it with hers. Her power overtakes mine as she lifts the two of us to level with Serafina and Brayden. She raises her free hand, sending a blast of energy into the duo. Serafina flies backward with the immortal child in her arms.

"Again," Brayden says through my mind. *"That weakened her."*

Nyssa repeats the move from before, throwing her back even further. "Put the boy down and fight," Aaron says from below.

I watch in horror as the witch's hand becomes transparent. Forcing Brayden in front of her, she punches her hand through his skin, grabbing hold of what I can only assume is his heart. His eyes roll back in his head as his mouth opens to a silent scream.

"Release the illusion," I beg through our connection. *"Please, Brayden. Don't do this. We can win."*

"No, you can't," his soft voice echoes. *"This is the only way. You need...Aaron."*

"You know," Serafina spews. "The only way to truly kill a vampire is to cut off their head or stake them through the heart.

"Stop!" I scream. "Nyssa, let me go." Nyssa ignores my request and sends another blast of our combined power into the witch.

"We're not strong enough," Nyssa says. Below us, Aaron has his grimoire open and is chanting in a language similar to the one Serafina used. "Brayden, we need you," she yells toward the tortured immortal child.

The void surrounding us begins to blink slightly, giving way to hints of the mansion and bayou before returning to the illusion. "That's it, baby. Let the illusion go," I encourage him.

"You see? Even in the illusion, I'm still stronger."

The void flashes away once more, long enough to catch a glimpse of Thorne standing on the perimeter. "Thorne?" I whisper. As soon as the blackness returns, it disappears once more. This time, giving enough time for Thorne to enter the void.

"Brother, dear. It's good to see you less crispy." I stare at the spectacle in front of me. I've never felt so out of control. Even in the bowels of Kragen's ship, I had control over myself. Now, with Nyssa using my power, Serafina holding Brayden's life in her fist, my brother casting spells beneath me, and Thorne still under his sister's influence, I can't fix this. I'm nothing more than a helpless participant trapped in a game with no winner.

Thorne flies into the air like it's something he's done his entire life. He moves to Serafina's side. "I'm here, sister."

"Kill them," she demands.

Thorne turns toward me, his pupils wide and dilated. He makes eye contact with me, saying more than his mouth ever could. Power floods me from inside, stronger than ever before. Without breaking eye contact with Thorne, I pull away from Nyssa and fly straight toward Serafina, praying that my instincts are right.

I move to Thorne's side as he turns toward his sister. "Someone will die today, but it won't be them." He grabs my hand, and a surge of power rushes through my body. Thorne sends the energy into the ancient witch, knocking her and Brayden to the ground below in a sickening thud.

Seconds later, we're on the ground next to them. Ignoring Serafina, I move toward Brayden. The illusion is still holding, which means he's alive.

"Brayden?" I pull him away from what remains of Serafina. Cradling his tiny body in my arms. "Brayden, you're going to be okay. I've got you."

Instead of fading in and out, the dome of the void begins to break apart, reminding me of a puzzle, falling apart one piece at a time.

"It's okay, Elsie." He pulls his hand away from his chest, revealing the wooden stake shoved through his tiny heart. "We did it."

I fight tears. "*You* did it."

He turns his tiny head toward Thorne, Nyssa, and Aaron. "We all did..." His eyes close, and the void disappears completely.

"Brayden!" I shout, pulling his tiny body into mine. "This wasn't supposed to happen."

I turn, finding the trio of remaining immortal children standing just on the other side of what was the perimeter of the void. They're filthy and covered in blood, but they're alive.

"He's gone," I whisper for their ears only.

"*We know. We felt him leave,*" Alex answers. I don't ask questions as the three of them move to Brayden's side, wrapping him in their arms and carrying him off the porch of the house.

"Where are you going?"

"We're taking him home." I don't question them as they carry his tiny body away from the carnage.

Beside me, the once-powerful ancient witch lies in a puddle of blood and remains. Her face is nearly unrecognizable, and what was her mouth is frozen in a perpetual scream. Other than Kragen, I've never been happier to see someone dead.

I turn toward the spot where Aaron was moments earlier. The only piece of him that remains is the grimoire that was the focus of all of this. "He's gone," I whisper. "They're both gone."

Thorne wraps his arms around me, pulling me to his chest. The feeling is familiar and welcome while I cry tears for Brayden, the boy who never had a chance to live, and for Aaron, the brother I never knew.

The chaos surrounding me is over as Cam runs to our side. He's in human form and naked, but as usual, he doesn't seem to notice or care. Blood drips from different places on his body, his or someone else's, I'm not sure, and he's covered in dirt and debris.

"Brayden?" he asks breathily.

"He's gone," Thorne answers. "The children took him."

Cam moves to Nyssa's side, who looks weaker than I've seen her before. He wraps an arm around her, pulling her close. "The children and I took care of the bound." He nods toward a pile of lycan bodies and what remains of the vampires. "Is it over?" he asks anyone who's listening.

"Aye," Thorne answers. "Serafina is dead."

"What now?" Cam asks as he and Nyssa move down the grand staircase.

"We live," he answers.

the aftermath of death

THE CLEANUP IS ALMOST as bad as the fight. Connor sent nearly the entire pack to get rid of the bodies. When Serafina died, so did her illusion. The antebellum home that she kept hidden in the shadows is now visible for all to see. The grandeur that was evident when we arrived is replaced by the aged remnants of a once majestic home, now nothing more than a facade of bricks and pillars.

The pack burns what remains of the bodies, making sure to pay their respects to each victim, even the vampires.

I've spent the past two hours sitting on the dilapidated stairs. Brayden's last minutes play through my mind on endless repeat. In the three centuries I've been alive, I've witnessed more death than I can count. Still, nothing prepared me to witness the immortal child's death.

"What do you think they're doing with his body?" I ask Fran, who's joined me.

"Most likely, there's nothing left at this point. He's returned to the dust from which he came."

"He was just a child." My words are barely audible. "A sweet, innocent child." Fran laces her fingers through mine. "Do you think there's someplace other than this?" I look around at the carnage.

"Are you asking if I think there's a heaven?" she asks.

"Aye. Maybe. Truthfully, I don't know what I'm asking. I just don't want it to be over for him."

Fran makes eye contact. "If there is something beyond this world, I have no doubt that Brayden is there."

"Do you think they allow vampires in?"

"Brayden was nothing but kind, even as a vampire. I grew to love him in the weeks he was with me. He's there, probably smiling down on us, telling us to get over these tears."

I laugh at the image she paints. "You're right. He wouldn't want us to cry over him." I sniff. "I'm going to think of him being with his parents."

"That's the only way we can think of him." She squeezes my fingers. "The pack wanted me to let you know they are finished and leaving." Fran stands, moving back down the stairs.

"Fran?" She turns back toward me. "Thank you."

She winks before leaving me alone. Cam and Nyssa

come around the corner of the house. Both look exhausted and are covered in a mixture of everything. I'm curious where Cam found a pair of shorts that almost fit him, but not enough to ask. "We're ready," Nyssa says.

"You and Cam go. We'll meet you there." Thorne appears out of nowhere, returning to his role as my protector. A role he's played since becoming a vampire.

"I'm going to go, too," Fran says, moving vampire speed next to the lycan. "Can I ride with you?"

"Of course," Cam answers, placing a heavy arm over her shoulders. "You were awesome out there." His encouragement to the older vampire is endearing.

Thorne sits beside me as we watch them leave the property. "Are you okay?" he asks once my friends are out of sight.

"I should be asking you that."

"Aye, I'm okay."

"What was it like?" I ask.

"What?"

"What was it like being under her control? Did you know what was happening?"

Thorne's quiet for a moment. "It was like playing a video game without the ability to control the character. I was here. I was aware of what I was doing, but I had no choice in my behavior."

"I'm sorry."

"Thank you, but you don't owe me an apology."

"Eudora's dead."

His eyebrows raise high on his forehead. "How?"

"It's a long story, but in a nutshell, she caught fire."

"Nice. Phyllis?"

"She died saving the children." I wipe a stray tear. "First Phyllis, now Brayden."

"Hopefully, the killing is over for a while." He pushes a lock of stray hair behind my ear. Why he chose just one out of all the hair that's gone crazy on my head, I don't know. "I hate to ask this, but what about Marnie?"

At the mention of Kragen and Eudora's daughter, my stomach flips. "Autumn said she was sent to another realm."

"What?" he asks, his forehead wrinkling with confusion.

I shrug. "I don't know, but I trust Autumn."

"Then the children will be safe."

"Did you know what you were saying?" I look down as I speak.

Thorne sighs, rubbing my thumb mindlessly with his. "Nothing I can say now will make up for the horrible things I said while under the binding." He closes his eyes. "I'm sorry, Elsie."

I wipe a stray tear. "Is that what you think of me? Were your words true?"

"No. I loved you from the moment I caught you stealing food from my chambers. You were strong, beautiful, and even as a nineteen-year-old starving human, you still had the qualities that make you the woman you are today."

"Your words came from somewhere," I retort.

"I never meant any of it. The words were there. It was nothing, I thought." He kisses the back of my hand. "I'll never stop trying to make it up to you."

I don't respond. He's right. Even though the words weren't his, the echoes replay through my mind. I stand, pulling him along with me. "I want to leave this place." I look at the dilapidated building. "Even with barely anything standing, and Serafina's illusion gone, it doesn't feel right. The energy is bad here."

"Aye." He looks into my eyes. "Burn it, acushla."

"It won't get rid of the energy."

"No, but it's a good start."

I close my eyes, allowing the energy to flow quickly. Without hesitation, I face the monstrosity. "Burn," I whisper. The remains burst into flames immediately. The ancient wood burns quickly as the fire makes its way throughout what's left of the facade.

The air smells of ash and charred wood as Thorne and I stand in the blackened ruins of the mansion, or what's left of it. The once-grand antebellum home is now nothing more than a graveyard of memories and secrets.

The four white pillars still stand, rising into the perfect summer sky. They're scorched, paint blistered and peeling, but they didn't fall. Instead, they stand like silent sentinels, guarding the empty space where walls and windows once stood.

"It's done," I whisper.

"Aye." Thorne laces his fingers through mine. "Now, we can go."

Moving away from the house, a stray beam of light catches my eye. Straight from what remains of the clouds, it shines in the middle of the remains. "Look," I point out the anomaly to Thorne.

"There's something in the light," he says, pulling away from my grip.

I follow him to the beam just as it disappears. Lying on the charred remains of the house is Aaron's grimoire. The edges are burned, and the rune that covers the front is impossible to recognize, but there's no doubt it's his grimoire.

"I watched most of it burn. How is that possible?"

"Magic," Thorne answers. I squat in front of the book, not sure if I should keep it or leave it to rot with the remains. A gust of wind from nowhere lifts the cover slightly as if someone is moving it on purpose. "I think he wants you to take it."

"Aaron?" I ask, looking around, half expecting him to appear out of thin air. Pulling the grimoire to my chest, I fight tears. Dammit, that's all I've done lately.

As soon as the book makes contact with the exposed skin on my chest, a burst of energy flows into me and back to the book again. The energy feels familiar–like family–like home.

"He's here," I whisper to Thorne. I shake the book for effect. "He's inside."

Instead of moving at the speed we're capable of, we walk at a human pace back to where the truck was parked earlier. The only thing remaining are tire tracks, which means Nyssa, Cam, and Fran should be at her home by now.

......

By the time we arrive back at Fran's Charleston home, the three of them are clean and wearing what I would classify as "comfy" clothes. "Any sign of the kids?" I ask the trio as we enter.

"Nothing," Fran answers. "Elsie, you need to be prepared. They may not return. They have their freedom and deserve their peace."

"I refuse to accept that. They'll return."

"Is that the grimoire?" Nyssa asks, changing the subject. "How? I watched it burn. We all watched it burn."

"Aye, it did. I think Aaron saved it."

"Aaron, your brother?" Fran asks.

"He was there. In the illusion that Brayden created —he was there." I fight the emotion filling my body.

"Without him, we wouldn't have been as strong," Nyssa adds.

"What happened outside the illusion?" I ask.

Cam leans forward, running a hand through his

still-wet hair. "The children. I've never seen anything like it. They worked as a team, a terrifying team, killing everything in their path."

"It's the reason immortal children are not allowed," Fran says with a far-off look on her face.

"Understandable," Cam answers.

"What's next?" I ask the small group.

"We go back to life as normal. Or at least as normal as it can be for people like us." Fran's words feel wise.

"I don't know what normal is," I add. "My life has been filled with running, hiding, death, and destruction." Thorne laces his fingers through mine, sending waves of strength through our connection.

"How did you come back so quickly?" Fran asks the man at my side. "It can take days for a vampire to come back from death. You should still be a charred body." Her words are harsh but true.

Thorne shrugs. "That's a good question, and one I don't have an answer for."

"The druid blood." Nyssa fills in the blank. "You are powerful, Thorne. That power will draw people to you, people who don't have good intentions. The ritual we performed was the catalyst for the druid to come to power."

"I'll be prepared," he answers.

"You need to be." Nyssa rubs her temples. "I will teach you everything I know, however, something tells me you'll teach me more." She stands. "If you'll excuse me. I need some sleep. My energy is drained."

"Mine, too." Cam joins her as they head upstairs together. I'm watching them ascend when what can only be described as an anomaly catches my attention. The top landing of the stairs glitches, turning into the familiar blackness of the void.

"Did you see that?" I ask, moving behind them in the blink of an eye.

"What?" Cam asks, turning toward me.

"The stairs. They...they disappeared."

"No," he answers. "Are they back?"

I laugh, not sure what just happened. "Yeah. I think it's safe. Sorry. My mind is a jumbled mess after today."

"Goodnight," Nyssa says as the two of them continue their trek, disappearing into the shadows of the home.

"I'm going up to take a shower." I stand, following the lycan.

Ten minutes later, the glory of the water scorches my skin, pulling some of the dread and sadness from the day away. Turning to wash the third batch of shampoo from my hair, the dark, ornate tile that surrounds the open shower disappears, turning into the same void as the landing. "What the hell?" I ask out loud to no one.

The void disappears as quickly as it appeared, leaving me more confused than before. Am I losing it? Can vampires go insane? My laugh echoes off the tile that has returned to line the walls. This is my cue to exit the shower.

I throw on a pair of oversized sweatpants I find in the wardrobe and the matching sweatshirt. My hair has stopped dripping but is still soaking wet as I make my way out toward the plush bed, and Aaron's awaiting grimoire. The door to my room creaks open, catching me by surprise.

"Are you okay?" Thorne asks the question he's asked at least ten times since our trip back to Fran's.

I open my mouth to answer the same way I have each time when the reality of what I witnessed hits me. "No," I whisper.

He climbs on top of the bed, wrapping his arms around me. "I'm sorry, acushla."

"You know it's not your job to keep me happy or safe?" I ask, pulling back slightly. "I appreciate your attempt, but it's not your job. I love you for everything you do. That will never change." I wipe a silent tear streaming down my cheek. "But I'm capable, Thorne. I always have been."

"I know. If it weren't for you, I'd still be under Serafina's influence."

"It wasn't me. It was Brayden, and now he's gone." My silent tears have gone to full-fledged tears, streaming down my cheek. "I failed him. I should've been able to save him."

"You can't take that on yourself, Elsie. You can't save everyone."

"I have to try!" Thorne doesn't respond. Instead, the look on his face mirrors mine as the realization of my trauma slaps us both in the face. I sacrificed my humanity to save everyone on Thorne's ship. I sacrificed my life on the run from Kragen. Holy shit...he's right. I don't have to save everyone.

I lean into his arms, burying my head into his chest. He gives me time to cry, keeping his arms around me the entire time. I pull away just as the entire room disappears, turning into the blackness of the void.

"What is this?" Thorne whispers, pulling away slightly.

"It's the void. The world Brayden created."

"Acushla, if Brayden created it, why are we here?"

A deep voice echoes from behind. "Because I brought you here." I turn, finding the now familiar face of Aaron. He's dressed in black and holding the grimoire. He steps in front of Thorne, holding his hand toward his former captain.

"Hawthorne Rex," Thorne introduces himself.

"We've met," Aaron answers with a smile.

"Not that I'm not happy to see you, brother, but how are you here?" I ask.

"I'm here because the void is cracking."

I stare at the image of my father. "What?"

He motions to the darkness around us. "This world is cracking."

"Brayden died. His illusion would die with him."

"It's not an illusion, sister. It's an endless world, blacker than night, with no ground, no sky, nothing to hold onto. You don't float or fall—you simply exist. It's not a place you see or touch—it's something you feel, something that feels *you*. It's the kind of nothing that tries to pull everything out of you, and if you stay too long, you might forget how to leave."

"What are you saying?"

"If it cracks, the world will be no more."

saving the world...again

"DO we really need anything else to be responsible for?" Nyssa asks. She and Cam got about two hours of sleep before Thorne, and I woke them to share the news. "Can't someone else save the world for once?" She yawns, running her hands through her normally perfect hair.

"I agree," Cam says, wandering around the room.

"What is a crack in the void?" Fran asks.

"Aaron explained that the crack was caused by the imbalance of the void," I try to explain, using my brother's words, hoping I do them justice. "When Brayden took Serafina to the void, I don't know if he realized it was a real place, not something he created. The void is not meant to be entered by anyone bound to the mortal or immortal planes. It exists as a neutral, timeless realm —a boundary rather than a destination. By bringing Serafina and us into the void, he introduced elements that didn't belong—her power, her emotions, her very essence.

"The void thrives on neutrality, but Serafina's presence, driven by her thirst for vengeance, disrupted that balance. Her energy rippled through the void, shifting neutrality. Brayden's druidic magic, tied to the earth and life, clashed with the void's emptiness, creating a volatile reaction, introducing forces that were never meant to coexist and, in turn, the barriers that keep it separate from the other realms."

"Basically, the imbalance was a consequence of two incompatible energies—Serafina's destructive power and Brayden's life-bound magic—forcing their way into a realm that exists outside the laws of their world." I pause, proud of myself for remembering most of his words. "Aaron said the void doesn't forgive disruptions. Instead, it shifts, reacts, and seeks to restore equilibrium, often at great cost."

"Holy shit. That was impressive," Cam says, wearing a huge smile on his face. "I felt like I just sat through a science lesson mixed with a little *woo-woo.*" He wiggles his fingers with his last words.

"Thank you?" I'm not sure how to respond to that. I give myself a metaphorical pat on the back.

"What happens if it cracks completely?" Nyssa asks.

"If the balance isn't restored, it will unravel the boundaries between realms, allowing chaos into creation. Mortal and immortal worlds would collide, the laws of time and space would fracture, and magic would become unstable and destructive."

"What do we do about it?" Fran asks the magic question—no pun intended.

"A spell," I answer, holding the grimoire tight to my chest. "Aaron says a spell will show itself for what we need."

Nyssa sighs. "Some grimoires have that ability." She looks up. "My energy is gone. Did Aaron give us a timeline?"

"He said the longer we wait, the more the void will crack."

"So, in other words, now," Cam answers.

"It's going to take all of us," I add.

"What if I'm not strong enough to help?" Nyssa asks. "I'm human for the most part. My body is tired. I don't know if I'll be much help right now."

"The children," Fran announces. "We need the children."

"Aye, but we don't know where they are."

"Call them, acushla," Thorne answers. "Call Alex. He'll come."

I fight the urge to argue that Alex deserves his life and freedom. His job isn't to save the supposed adults, but Thorne is right. We need them. I close my eyes. *"Alex?"* I'm met with nothing in return. *"Alex? We need you. I need you."* Several minutes pass with no response. I try one more time. *"Alexander, answer me."*

"Elsie, I hear you. What's wrong?"

Relief fills me at the sound of his voice. *"The void is cracking, and we need to fix it."*

I'm met with silence on the other end for several minutes. *"What does that even mean?"* he asks, making me laugh. Thorne, Nyssa, and I spend the next few minutes explaining what the void is and how we need to fix it. I repeat Aaron's words, hoping to do them justice.

"How can we help with that?" he asks.

"By lending your powers." He's quiet for longer than before. *"Autumn, Everly, I know you can hear me. I'm so sorry for Brayden. He was braver than anyone I've ever met. He saved us all. It's our job now. We need to fix this and continue what he started. I loved him, and I love you."*

"We're on our way," Everly's soft voice answers.

·······

True to their word, the children's energy reaches me a few hours later. "They're here," Thorne announces before I do. A soft knock on the door follows his words.

I open the door a heartbeat later, not caring that it's not my home. Alex, flanked by his sisters, stands at the door. "We're here," Alex says.

"Aye, you are." I step back. "Please, come in."

The immortal children enter, bringing an energy that feels different than before. "Are you alright?" I ask. My question is horrible. How could they be okay?

"It's okay, Elsie. Your question isn't horrible." Alex

turns toward Thorne. "We buried what was left of him."

"What?" Nyssa asks.

"Thorne wanted to know where Brayden is." Alex moves further into the house, his sisters remaining at his sides.

"I'm sorry." I look each of them in the eyes with my words.

"So are we," Autumn answers.

"What power do you think we can provide to heal the void?" Everly, always the most serious of all of them, asks.

"The three of you hold magic in your blood. It's why you're able to do the things you do," Nyssa answers.

"You mean we're not uncontrollable monsters." Autumn fills in the blanks. I stare at the immortal children, not sure why they seem different than before. I'm contemplating asking when Alex interrupts my thoughts.

"We've decided we want to live on our own," he answers my unasked question. "We're capable and ready."

"I think that's a great idea," Fran answers. "You know you're always welcome here should you change your minds."

"Thank you, Fran," Alex answers. "We will keep that in mind."

"What do we need to do?" Autumn asks. "We're here to help."

Pulling the grimoire in front of me, I open it to a blank page. "There is a spell that will help us heal the void."

"That page is blank," Everly states the obvious.

"Aye, but it won't be," I answer.

"Set the grimoire in the middle of the floor," Nyssa announces, taking the leadership position. "In order for this to work, everyone has to open themselves and freely release their power."

"How do you know what to do?" Cam asks.

"I don't," she answers. "I'm going purely off instinct."

"That's better than nothing," he adds.

"Form a circle and hold hands. Elsie, go to the grimoire, and we'll circle you," Nyssa continues her instructions. I do as she says, kneeling in front of the singed book while the rest form a small circle surrounding me. "Open it."

The book seems to hear her words and responds without much effort from me. A blank page looks back at me as I stare into the heavy grimoire. The energy shifts as Nyssa begins chanting in a familiar yet unfamiliar language.

Mimicking her words, I send my energy into the grimoire, willing it to show the spell I need. The energy surrounding me is palpable. Every hair on my body stands at attention. The feeling reminds me of the moment before a lightning strike, when inanimate objects seem to take on a life of their own, waiting for the strike that's about to come.

The children, Fran, and Cam join the chanting until faint writing begins to form on the page. Several minutes later, the words completely form, filling the page with the familiar penmanship found throughout the grimoire. Silence surrounds me.

"Read the spell, Elsie," Nyssa says from her place in the circle.

Moving closer, I begin to read the words aloud. "From the depths of chaos to the edges of creation, we call upon the forces of balance and restoration. With earth, fire, water, and air, we mend the tear and repair the despair.

"Through blood and bond, through power and pain, let harmony rise, and chaos wane. Void of shadow, light, and strife, we return to thee the breath of life.

"By our will, let balance be restored. By our sacrifice, the realms be moored. Bound by the ancient, sealed by the new, void, be healed—we summon you true."

I finish the spell and sit in silence. I'm not sure whether I expect a sonic boom or something a little more subtle, but when nothing happens, I'm convinced it didn't work. I wait a few minutes before interrupting the silence. "Nyssa? Did it work?"

"I don't think so," she answers. I glance at the druid lycanthrope to see the room behind her disappear into darkness. This time, the fracture is larger than the ones I witnessed earlier. It covers most of the room, changing the energy with it.

"No," I confirm. "It didn't work. What did I do wrong?"

"You have to believe it, Elsie," Everly says. "You have to become one with the words."

I hold my hand toward the immortal child who has the ability to mimic others' power. "Help me, Everly. Can you mimic Brayden's power?"

"I think so," she whispers.

"Do it."

She doesn't argue. Moving to my side, we join hands, surrounding the grimoire that lies between us. "Cast the spell again," Alex says. "It's going to take all of your power."

"Say it with me?" I ask the immortal child in front of me. She nods, and we begin to recite the spell again, this time in unison. With her boost of power, the energy is stronger this time. Energy fills my body as we finish the spell. On our last word, the room explodes in what reminds me of a blast wave, echoing through the room, knocking down furniture, and exploding windows as it exits.

Everly and I are breathing way harder than vampires should. "Did we do it?" she asks. Her soft voice filling the silent room.

"Yes," Nyssa answers. "I can feel it. The void has been mended."

"Aye. Me, too," Thorne adds. "I don't know how, but I can feel the balance."

"The druid blood in you feels it," Nyssa answers.

"Well, damn. What is it with my homes and windows?" Fran props her hands on her hips. "Why didn't we go outside?"

"We saved the world for the second time today, and you're worried about windows?" Cam's words are meant to tease rather than chastise the older vampire.

"That's a good point," she agrees. "Good job, ladies and gentlemen."

"Now what?" Cam asks. "Is that it?"

"That's it," Nyssa answers. "Now we rest." She sits down heavily, more drained than before.

Cam joins her. "I'm worn out, and I didn't contribute magical powers."

I turn toward Alex. "Thank you." I wrap my arms around him, pulling him close.

Small arms wrap around my waist as he buries his head into my abdomen. "You want to know if we're going to stay or leave."

I sigh before answering. "It's rude to listen to others' thoughts," I remind him. He smiles widely with our familiar banter. "You are welcome to stay with me." I look between the children. "All of you are welcome to stay."

"We know," Autumn answers. "We've decided we want to be like Celeste—adults."

"We're going to search for someone to help us," Everly adds.

"I can help you," Fran confirms, moving to our side. She closes her eyes for longer than usual. "It's not easy. Celeste dealt with unimaginable pain, and you know the consequence she paid. She's no longer immortal."

"We're ready," Alex answers, pulling away from my embrace.

"Yeah, immortality isn't all it's cracked up to be." The simplicity of Autumn's words lightens the energy remaining in the room.

"Stay with me. Celeste and I will put you in contact with people who can help you." Fran smiles.

"Thank you, Fran," the children answer in unison.

"On one condition," Fran adds. "You have to stop doing that. Answering in unison is creepy." The children laugh, lightning the energy even more.

"I can't imagine you as adults." I look each child in the eye as a tear falls from mine. "Each of you holds a special place in my heart. In the short amount of time we've known each other, we've lived lifetimes full of adventure."

"Aye," Thorne adds, ruffling the perfectly styled hair on Alex's head. My mind flashes back to the immortal child, forced to find food for his siblings and terrorized by *Mother*, his maker. If anyone deserves to grow and escape his reality, it's him. It's all of them.

"Thank you, Fran."

"Yes, thank you." The children surround the elderly

vampire. In a horror movie, this would be terrifying. In our world, it's normal.

Thorne wraps a long arm around my waist, and the two of us work our way upstairs. "Elsie?" Alex calls. I turn, making eye contact with my favorite immortal child. He holds his hand in front of him, opening his fingers slowly. "Brayden wanted you to have this."

"Me?" I'm back in front of him in the blink of an eye. Nestled in his palm is a beautiful blue crystal. The stone resonates with energy.

"This is from Brayden?"

"Yes. He carried it in his pocket even before he was a vampire."

I take the token from his hand, rubbing my fingers over the smooth edges of the stone. "It's beautiful."

"It's powerful," Nyssa says from the stairs. "I feel its energy from here."

"How do you know he wanted me to have it?" Instead of answering, Alex taps his temples, letting me know he used his power. "Thank you." Closing my fingers around it, the energy of love and joy fills me immediately.

true love

SITTING on the edge of the bed, I find myself staring at Brayden's gift. The crystal's blue is almost other-worldly—an iridescent hue that seems to shift and shimmer beyond words. It's as if the color exists between dimensions, both vibrant and muted, dark yet translucent. At times, it almost feels alive. Then, in an instant, it softens, rippling with shades of blue as if the color itself is...breathing.

"It's beautiful," Thorne says, interrupting whatever the hell I'm doing.

"Aye. It is." I close my fingers around the crystal, breaking the invisible spell it's placed me under. "I feel like it's more than just a beautiful crystal."

"Knowing the kid, it probably is."

I place the crystal on the nightstand and turn toward the man I've loved for what seems like forever.

"I was scared." Thorne turns his full attention toward me as I admit something I've never admitted before.

"It's okay, acushla."

"I need to say this." I swallow the heavy lump in my throat. A very human action for a vampire. "For the first time since finding you again, I was scared you would die." Saying the words out loud sounds even more vulnerable than I imagined. Thorne is the only person I would ever open myself up to. "I couldn't bear losing you. I've lost everyone that's ever meant anything to me." I scoff. "Gods, that sounded so selfish. I'm sorry, Thorne."

"Don't apologize."

"I should've come after you sooner."

Strong fingers link into mine. "Elsie, stop. Everything happened the way it needed to happen. The children needed to be free from Eudora, who needed to leave this world. If you had come after me without them, you wouldn't have been strong enough to defeat Serafina. Everything happens for a reason. Sometimes we don't know why, sometimes we do."

"How are you so smart?"

He shrugs. "I know I can never take back the things I said while..." I place my index finger on his lips, stopping his words.

"I know. You were under Serafina's binding. They weren't your words."

"I love you, acushla." He leans over, kissing me on the forehead. "I've missed your forehead."

I laugh at his admission. "I've never thought of my forehead as being my best feature."

"It's one of my favorites. So is this." He leans down further, kissing my cheek.

"What about these? Have you missed them?" I gently rub my index finger over my gloss-covered lips.

"I've missed those the most." He gently places his lips on mine. His kisses are gentle. Soft pecks on my quickly swollen lips. Thorne's callused hand moves to my cheek, rubbing his thumb across the skin, offering both comfort and heat with his touch. My breath catches as his kisses become more aggressive than before. A soft moan forces my lips apart, and he takes advantage by pushing his tongue inside. The moment our tongues connect, heat explodes throughout my body. I've lost track of how much time has passed since we've had the opportunity to enjoy each other.

Reaching between the seams on his shirt, I don't waste time unbuttoning. I rip the shirt, exposing his rigid chest. Running my hands over each ab, I relish the feel under my fingertips. "I've missed you," I whisper into his mouth. "I've missed us."

Thorne slides his hand under the hem of my shirt, slowly making his way to the tip of my breast. A second breath catches as his thumb rubs the nub that's swollen with desire. I'm quickly becoming his thumbs' number one fan.

"Is this okay?" he asks, pulling the edge of the shirt toward my head.

"It's more than okay." The casual speed of my shirt removal gets on my nerves. Reaching past his hand, I rip the cotton nearly in half, pulling the shreds over my head. Thorne's laugh is deep, doing even more things to me.

"I've missed this." He sighs. I reach around, unlatching the bra that's been holding my breasts in place. Thorne's pupils grow slightly at the sight of my bare chest.

I place a hand on each of his shoulders and push him back to the bed. "I've missed this," I answer, kissing his neck and slowly working my way down to the belt holding his jeans in place. Instead of the speed I used to remove my shirt and bra, I move purposefully slow, unlatching the leather and the clip holding the belt. The bulge under his jeans lets me know I'm not the only one ready to go.

Straddling his hips, I unbutton and unzip the jeans just as slowly as the belt. Even though it's not necessary for a vampire to breathe, Thorne's chest is rising and falling much faster than normal. "If you don't hurry," he sighs, "I'm—" He stops.

"You'll what?"

Without warning, he flips, putting me underneath him and pressing the hardest part of him into just the right spot. "I'll do this," he answers breathlessly just before he takes my nipple into his mouth. While his tongue assaults one nipple, his hand takes care of the other. Rolling, twisting, and sucking. The trifecta of enjoyment. My hips rise to meet him, matching the tempo of his fingers.

"Elsie." He sighs. I don't wait for Thorne. Reaching between us, I pull the borrowed sweatpants I'm wearing down along with the thin pair of panties underneath. He pulls back, admiring my body and making me more self-conscious than usual. "You're beautiful."

My normal snarky response is cut short by Thorne sliding down my chest and stomach, leaving a trail of kisses along the way. He works his way to the exact spot I want him, and my breath catches. "Spread your legs," he demands—his voice deep.

I do as he says, pulling my knees as far to the side as possible. He slides down, resting his shoulders on my thighs. The moment his tongue makes contact, I squirm under the connection. He slowly slides his tongue in all the right places, stopping on the part that's begging to be touched. "Is this what you want?"

"Yes."

"Tell me what you want me to do."

"Touch me."

"Tell me, acushla." He teases my clit with his tongue, pulling away seconds later.

"I want..." He teases me again, taking my words away.

"Tell me." I arch my hips, trying to reach his mouth. He moves, evading my attempts. "Tell me, Elsie."

"Make me cum." I pant, gripping his head with my

hands. He gives in, sucking my clit into his mouth and rubbing the tip of his tongue against the pulsing body part. He doesn't stop there. His fingers are inside of me, seconds later, finding the perfect spot to rub.

Our connection hits without warning. My body melts into butter under his touch as my legs begin to shudder. "Cum for me, baby," he says between assaults.

He doesn't have to tell me again. My body is refusing any other options. One last tongue and finger rub in unison, and my body explodes in a loud burst of uncontrolled passion. Undoubtedly, everyone in the house is a witness to what I just experienced, and I'm not the least bit embarrassed. My body continues to tingle under his touch until I push him away to recover. "That was perfect," I whisper.

"I love seeing you like that." Thorne's eyes are wide with desire. Stealing his earlier move, I wrap my legs around his thighs, flipping both of us. With him on the bottom, I begin to slowly grind my hips. "Elsie," he growls.

I pull back. "Did you just growl at me?"

"Aye. You're doing things to me that I can't control."

I move inches from his ear. "Do you want me to stop?"

"Don't you dare."

Sitting up, I shimmy the unbuckled and unzipped jeans down his hips to the top of his thighs. "It's your turn." I lean forward, kissing each one of the muscles, and working my way up to his lips. Taking his lower lip between my teeth, I bite just enough to draw a small trickle of blood.

"Ouch." He breathes into my mouth. "I liked that."

"Then you're going to really like this." The moan he lets out encourages me as I run my body against the length of him—teasing him. I repeat the motion, this time leaving enough room for my hand to guide him where I want him. Lining us up, I lower myself slowly. The sensation of him filling me nearly pushes me over the edge. Lacing my fingers through his, I force his hands to his sides, lowering my body completely and leaving no space between us.

"Acushla," he murmurs. Sliding up and down, I continue moving while holding him in place. I cover his lips with mine, moving my hips in tempo with my tongue. The sensation I now recognize as my ability begins to build deep in my core. Ignoring the nagging energy, I continue my assault on Thorne. His sighs urge me to keep going.

Without warning, he pulls his arms free of my hold and wraps them around my hips. Energy flows through our connection and joins with what's in my core. "Fuck," he whispers. Strong fingers grasp my hips as the tension between us builds more than anything I've felt before.

We explode in unison, and our magic collides, igniting something between us. Something magical. Shockwaves flutter through my body, our energies spiraling together until it's impossible to tell where I end and he begins. The air around us hums, charged with power like the universe is holding its breath along with me.

"Thorne," I breathe. "Did you feel that?"

"Aye. I don't know what it was, but I'm a fan."

Waiting for my breath to slow down before rolling to Thorne's side. We lay in silence for a while, enjoying each other's energy.

"What now?" I ask.

"I'm okay with doing that again."

I punch him gently in the arm. "I mean with life. Now that we've saved the world a few times, I'm not sure what the future holds."

Thorne's deep laugh echoes off the wooden walls. "The way things seem to go, I'm sure we'll have the opportunity again...probably tomorrow."

"Elsie," a whisper wisps through my mind.

"Aye?" I answer.

"I said, the way things seem to go..."

"No. After that, you called my name."

"Elsie." I hear it again. This time, the timbre of the voice is different.

"One of the kids must be calling me. Can you hear it?"

Thorne shakes his head. "No. My head is blissfully silent."

"Alex, Everly, Autumn? Is one of you calling me?"

"No," Alex answers for the group.

"Elsbeth." I hear the call again.

"You seriously don't hear that?" I ask Thorne. He shakes his head. I'm out of bed and dressed a heartbeat later. An overwhelming desire to find the grimoire hits, refusing to be ignored.

"Where are you going?"

"To the grimoire." Thorne is up and dressed a second later. The two of us move downstairs, finding the book exactly where I left it, in Fran's private office/library. Moving closer, the energy flowing from it is stronger than I've felt before. "Do you feel that?"

"Aye. It feels…alive."

The rune burned from the front has reappeared and fills the charred remains of the once-solid cover. Lying my hand on top, I feel the magic of Aaron's work flow through me.

"Open it," Thorne whispers. "It wants you to."

Opening the book to no specific page, I'm surprised to see most of the previously blank pages are now full of Aaron's perfect script. "It's nearly full."

A folded piece of parchment paper falls to the floor. "That wasn't there before." Picking it up, the name across the top surprises me. "It's for me—from Aaron."

"I'll give you some time." Thorne moves toward the door.

"No. Please stay. This involves both of us."

Tears fill my eyes at the greeting neatly written across the top. "My dearest, Elsbeth," I whisper. "If you're reading this, it means the time has come for you to embrace the power that has always been yours. I know this path isn't easy...magic rarely is. It demands patience, courage, and the willingness to see yourself for who you truly are.

"The grimoire you hold is not just a book—it's a legacy. One that I leave in your hands with full confidence that you will honor it. Learn from it. Grow with it. And, most importantly, trust yourself. Magic is not about perfection. It's about connection to the world, to others, and to yourself.

"You are stronger than you know, Elsie. The trials you face are not meant to break you—they are meant to refine you. You've already proven that you can rise above pain, loss, and even death itself. What is magic compared to that?

"Take your time. Be patient with yourself. When the world feels heavy and the magic seems impossible to control, remember who you are.

"You are not alone in this, and you never will be. My love and my guidance are with you, even now. Remember, I'll see you in the shadows. With all my heart, Aaron." My voice cracks as I read his name. To think the infant that I was afraid wouldn't survive the trip to Charles Town, turned into a man with this much wisdom, is nearly overwhelming.

"I love you, too, Aaron," I whisper.

I HATE RUFFLES

"IS it really necessary for me to wear this god-awful dress?" I ask the small crowd gathered around me. "I haven't worn this much fabric in three hundred years."

"Quit complaining, Elsie," Fran says, zipping me into the fabric torture chamber. "You're going to look beautiful. Just roll with the flow and let it happen for once. You can't be in control of everything."

"Whatever." I scoff. I sound like a bratty teenager, rather than the centuries-old vampire I am.

Fran steps back from her creation, covering her mouth with her hand. "I was right. You look beautiful."

"I don't feel beautiful. I feel like a stuffed hog." I fluff the oversized skirt, hoping it helps make my point.

"It's perfect," Nyssa says, coming into the room. "You're going to be a showstopper."

"She's grumpy," Fran warns with a smile.

"I'm grumpy because I'm wearing twenty yards of fabric. Can we take this off now?"

Fran has me unzipped and free from bondage seconds later. "You might want to hurry. The guests should be arriving soon."

"Thank you," I answer, changing my tone instantly. Truthfully, I've become so dependent on Fran that I can't imagine not having her around. She's been splitting her time between Charleston and New Orleans while helping everyone and everything. We all owe her a debt of gratitude.

A familiar energy hits me in the gut, stopping Fran and me in our tracks. "What?" Nyssa asks, looking between the two of us. She looks around quickly. "Do I need to be ready to fight?"

"I don't think so," I answer, moving vampire speed out of my bedroom and to the front door. I open the door just before the man on my welcome rug rings the bell.

"Elsie," he says, taking my breath away.

"Oh, my gods." I look the man up and down. "You... you are gorgeous." I don't wait for an invitation. I wrap my arms around him in an instant, pulling him close to my body. Energy passes between the two of us.

"You can let me go now." His deep voice resonates through my mind.

I pull back, wiping a stray tear. "Alex, I'm so proud of you and...I'm speechless."

"That's a first," a girl says, stepping from behind him. Long blonde curls hang to her sides, and the smile that covers her face is one I'd recognize at any age.

"Autumn?" I rush to her, copying my motions from Alex. Her energy floods me in an instant. "You were hiding your energy?"

"Yeah. Well, we didn't hide it." She turns toward a young woman standing by the gate. "We had a little help."

"Everly?" I can't hide the tears that flow down my face. The last time I saw the immortal children, they were just that, children. Now, standing in front of me are three adults. Each is grown and beautiful in their own way.

"It's me," she says with a smile.

"Why do I feel like a mom whose kids just came home from college?"

"Because you're older than dirt," Alex answers.

"Not quite, but I'm older than you." I step away from the doorframe. "Please, come in." The trio follows me into the large colonial-style house, through the piazza, and into the open foyer. "Nyssa! Thorne! Fran!" I call into the house.

"They know we're here," Alex confirms. "They wanted to give you a first glance."

Fran and Thorne appear at my sides with Nyssa running down the stairs moments later. "Oh, my gods. Look at the three of you." Fran manages to hug all three children at the same time. She steps back, looking each one of them up and down. "You are gorgeous. All of you."

"Thank you," Autumn answers. Her blonde hair is styled perfectly, flowing away from her angular face. "You all look the same."

"Were there any...consequences?" Fran asks.

The trio shares a look. "No. Celeste was able to put us in contact with a practitioner who didn't require anything of us other than money."

"I'm so happy for you all," Fran says, wiping a tear.

"When does this party get started?" Everly asks. "I haven't had the chance to attend a wedding as an adult. Hell, not ever."

"Tonight," Nyssa answers. "The backyard is set up for the small group that's invited."

The doorbell rings, drawing my attention to a new energy. One that I recognize instantly. "Amelia, Topher, and the baby are here," I announce.

Fran beats me to the door, greeting her familiar friends. Ignoring the adults, she takes baby Edon, who is almost as large as his hybrid mother, into her arms. "Oh, Edon. Grandma Fran has missed you so much."

The redheaded boy laughs and hugs her around the neck. "Nana Fran," he says with a smile.

"When did he start talking?" I ask, welcoming them.

"Last month. He went from grunts and points to full-fledged sentences and paragraphs in one day."

Amelia sets the heavy baby bag on a chair next to the door. "I have a feeling he's going to keep me busy."

"Nana Fran doesn't care. Edon can come over to my house anytime he chooses." Fran's singsong voice fills me with joy.

"Don't say that too loud. I might take you up on it."

Topher lifts his nose into the air. "I smell my brother. Where is he?"

"Here," Cam says, coming from another room in the house. "You have no room to talk." He sniffs the air dramatically. "Can you even smell yourself?"

The two men embrace, throwing muscled arms around each other. "Congratulations, brother."

"Thanks," Cam answers.

"Zeke will be here in about an hour. His flight was held up at the airport."

"What about Celeste?" Fran asks.

"What about Celeste?" a soft voice says from the open door. Behind the now large crowd gathered in the foyer is Amelia's twin and a lycan I don't recognize.

"Oh, my gods. This is more than I can handle." Fran rushes to Celeste's side, wrapping her arms around the daughter she raised. She turns to the lycan, wrapping her arms around him. "Jasper, it's so good to see you."

"You, too, Fran." He hugs her back.

"Does anyone else realize how much supernatural power is in this foyer?" Nyssa asks, looking around the room.

"Enough to destroy a city," Topher says with a

smile. "Don't get any ideas, kids." He gives the immortal children a look that only a father can perfect.

"Whatever, old man," Alex answers. My mind flashes back to the little boy who was terrified, abused, and a killer. To see him now brings tears to the surface once more.

"I can read your thoughts," Alex says, interrupting my pity fest. "I wasn't a killer." He wraps his arms around my neck, kissing my forehead.

"I'm not used to you being this tall."

"Yeah, me, neither."

"I've taken the liberty, even though this is Elsie and Thorne's house, to assign each of you a room. You'll find your names on the doors. Please make yourselves at home. The wedding will take place at six," Fran announces to the group. "You'll find everything you need in your rooms."

The group disbands, following each other up the grand staircase and into their respective rooms. I watch as they disappear around the corner. Thorne senses my mixture of emotions and wraps his arm around my shoulders.

"Everything's going to be alright, acushla."

"I know."

......

Three hours later, I'm covered in fabric for the

second time today. "Let the record state that I wouldn't wear all of these ruffles for anyone else."

Thorne's deep laugh echoes through our room. "You won't be the only one." He steps out of the bathroom wearing an outfit that draws me back to the nineteen-year-old girl traveling to America on his ship and the first night I saw him.

He stands tall, his coat a deep weathered blue with brass buttons catching the faintest light. Beneath it, a burgundy waistcoat hugs his frame, covering a linen shirt hanging open at the collar.

"Oh, my gods," I whisper.

"Too much?"

"No. Never. Just brings back memories."

"Aye, for me, too. Whose idea was it to dress for our time period?"

"Nyssa. No doubt for her own personal enjoyment."

Thorne holds his bent elbow to his side. "Shall we?"

I latch my arm through his. "We shall." We exit our room, heading downstairs. I have to concentrate way more than I should to get both me and the dress down the stairs in one piece. Waiting at the bottom is the trio of immortal children.

Alex is wearing a pinstripe suit straight out of the 1920s. His dark hair is slicked back, and he's leaning on a cane for effect. "You look amazing," I whisper, kissing him on the cheek.

"I prefer the word dapper."

Autumn grabs onto his arm, wearing a poodle skirt and iconic 1950s clothing. "I'm glad I never had to wear crinoline. This sucks."

"You look adorable, either way."

"That's what I told her," Everly says, grabbing Alex's other arm. She's wearing a pair of straight-legged jeans, rolled at the ankle; an oversized, brightly colored sweatshirt; and a pair of high-top Converse.

"You look like an MTV video," I say with a smile.

"Yeah, I feel like an MTV video."

"You two look really cool," Alex says, moving closer to Thorne. "This is awesome. I'm loving dressing from our time periods."

"Yeah, speak for yourself, but thank you." Thorne motions toward the back doors of the house. "Shall we?"

The once-immortal children follow us through the large double back door into the perfectly decorated backyard. Thorne escorts me down the aisle to the first row of seats. Alex, Autumn, and Everly join me as we wait for tonight's festivities.

A few minutes later, more guests begin arriving. I lose count of the number of lycan that join, all sitting on the opposite side of the aisle. Topher escorts Amelia and Edon down the aisle, seating them next to us before heading back into the house. He comes back with Celeste on his arm, not long after, sitting her next to her twin.

"It's about to start," he whispers as he retreats down the aisle one more time.

"I like your dress," Amelia says with a smirk.

"Pfft." I scoff. "I'm only doing this for Nyssa."

"Elsie?" Nyssa's voice echoes through my mind.

"Nyssa? Aren't you supposed to be walking down the aisle?"

"I need you."

I don't hesitate. I move slower than I normally would but faster than a human, into the house and into her room. "Are you okay?"

She wipes a tear from her cheek. "I don't know."

"Do you not want to go through with this? I can send everyone home."

"No, that's not it." She stands up straighter. "I don't have anything blue."

"What?"

"You know. Something old, something new, something borrowed, something blue."

"I've never heard that in my life, and I've lived a long life." I look around her room for something that will work. I spot a bright blue pencil on the corner of her dresser. "Here. Will this work?"

"Not really. I'm sorry. I realize this is dumb. It's just that when I thought about this day, I imagined it would be perfect."

"And something blue will make it perfect?"

"Goddess, I'm dumb."

I stare at the woman who has quickly become my

best friend. "I have something perfect. I'll be right back." I return a heartbeat later. Opening my hand, I reveal the perfect blue item.

"No," Nyssa argues. "That was meant for you."

"I don't think Brayden would mind you using it for a while."

She takes the flawless blue crystal from my hand. The energy that flashes through the room as she touches it is confirmation. Nyssa wipes her cheek, leaving a small streak of mascara in her wake. "This is perfect."

"Aye." I reach for the makeup brush on her counter, rubbing it across the smear. "You look beautiful."

"Thank you, Elsie." Moving toward the window, I see the entire wedding party in place. Thorne is standing at the foot of the aisle, with Cam next to him. Topher stands behind his baby brother, his hand protectively on his shoulder.

"It's time." I offer her my arm, and the two of us walk downstairs and to the back door.

"Will you walk me down?"

I turn toward my friend. "Are you sure? You were so adamant that you were coming down alone."

"Yeah, I've changed my mind." She looks at the lycan side of the garden. "There are a lot of wolves out there."

"Nyssa, you went through a mating ceremony, for God's sake. This is nothing."

"I know. Walk me down and hush."

She takes my arm once more, and the two of us exit the house, heading toward the sexy sea captain. "You're about to be married by the hottest vampire in existence," I whisper. Thorne smiles at my words.

"Thank you all for indulging me with the costumes."

"Yeah, you owe me." I take her to the end of the aisle, where Cam is already wiping tears.

"You look beautiful, my mate," he says for her ears only.

"Who gives this woman away?" Thorne asks.

I wrinkle my forehead. "Umm, me?"

The crowd surrounding us laughs as I work my way back to my seat to be an observer, not a participant. The ceremony doesn't take long as Thorne moves through the process of joining them as one. "Cameron St. James and Nyssa Jamison, I now pronounce you husband and wife. Cam, you may now kiss your bride."

I watch in awe as two of my closest friends become one. The weight of this moment isn't lost on me. The Elsie who spent two centuries running from her maker is not the same woman sitting here today. That Elsie was angry, ruthless, lashing out to spread the pain she carried. She thought she was punishing the world, but in the end, she was only hurting herself.

This Elsie—she sees the world differently now. There will always be cruelty and darkness, but I've learned that I get to choose where I stand. I can dwell in the shadows or reach for the light. And for the first time in my life, I am truly in control of me.

As Cam escorts Nyssa up the aisle, Alex reaches over, lacing his fingers through mine. No doubt, he heard my thoughts. *"I love you."* I send his way, squeezing his hand slightly.

"I love you, too. Thank you for being my light."

Madalyn Rae is the pen name for an author who loves telling a story. As a teacher of tiny humans during the day and author by night, she hopes she's able to draw you into her world of fantasy, make-believe, and love, even for a brief moment.

She lives on the Gulf Coast's beautiful white, sandy beaches, with her two loyal yet mildly obnoxious dogs, Whiskey and Tippi. She's the mother of two amazing adult children, a son-in-law, and a beautiful new grandson.

When not teaching or pretending to write, Madalyn is immersed in the world of music. Whether playing an instrument or singing a song, she is privileged to know that music is the true magic of the universe.

Magical Midlife Series

Season of Bone and Blood-Book 1

Season of Storm and Ash-Book 2

Witches of New Orleans-YA Novella Series

Haunted Hexes-Book 1

Christmas Brew-Book 2

Vampires of Charleston

Voyage of Death and Desire-Book 1

Voyage of Fury and Fate-Book 2

Voyage of Magic and Malice-Book 3

Vampires of New Orleans Series

Garden of the Past-Prequel Novella

Garden of Secret and Shadow-Book 1

Garden of Mystery and Intrigue -Book 2

Garden of Discovery and Love- Book 3

Ravenwood-Book 4

Garden of Rage and Ruin-Book 5

Morally Gray Novella Series

Full Moon Christmas

Nipping at Your Nose

Fallen

Lucky

The Elementals Series

Birth of the Phoenix-Adria's Novella-Prequel

Phoenix of the Sea- Book 1

Guardian of the Sea- Murphy's Novella

Ashes of the Wind- Book 2

Embers of the Flame-Keegan's Novella

Fire of the Sky-Book 3

The Elementals Collection-Box Set

The Elementals Collection

www.ingramcontent.com/pod-product-compliance
Lightning Source LLC
Chambersburg PA
CBHW031141160726

47991CB00004B/1510